SIERRALEON

Darrick Calvin

Dedication

This book is dedicated to my family for encouraging me to begin writing, to my friends for pushing me to publish my writing and poetry, and to you, my readers, for being open-minded and joining me on this journey.

Acknowledgment

I would like to express my gratitude to the people who have encouraged, pushed, or even threatened me to write. First and foremost, I want to thank my Ya-Ya for teaching me that it's okay to think differently and to take pride in my family. To my little big brother, thank you for being a constant presence in my life and for motivating me to strive for greatness. My heartfelt appreciation goes out to my kids, who have not only made me a better man but also a dedicated father, always inspiring me to pursue my dreams. I love and cherish each of you dearly.

Next, I want to extend my thanks to my friends. To those in school who have encouraged me to continue writing as a means of self-expression and stress relief, I am truly grateful. To my fellow Marine brothers and sisters who, after reading my adventurous works during deployments, pushed me to publish at least one book for them, thank you for your unwavering support. And to my friends in the Marine Corps, Army, and Navy who have guided me towards achieving my goal of getting my works published, your assistance has been invaluable. I hope you're all pleased now that the first book has been published.

Lastly, I want to express my deepest appreciation to you, the readers, for embracing my work. Thank you for engaging with it, whether by disagreeing, shedding tears, finding inspiration for the bedroom, or eagerly turning the pages to discover who emerged victorious. Your

support means the world to me.

Contents

Chapter 1

Yes, ma'am.

……Cloven........ □........(1).....

Rico Cloven heard the bath water running, so he went to the downstairs bathroom, where he found 7-year-old Leon looking at the water.

"Lee-Lee, I thought I told you to go to bed about 30 minutes ago," Rico asked.

"Yes, sir," Leon said without taking his attention off the water, "but Daddy, I must wet these big towels."

"Okay, Lil man, you go to bed, and I'll wet them for you, thank you, Daddy, good night," Leon said as his voice faded, Rico's eyes opened. His dream ended abruptly as he looked up to his clock that read 5:29.

At 5:30, the alarm went off. Rico stopped the alarm as he got up and prepared his book bag, running gear, shoes, and Koogler smart device for this morning's run. To his advantage, it had begun to rain, so he would be invisible to most. This run was to do a quick safety inspection of all the homes in this neighborhood, making sure all was good to go. He was also reviewing and finding new escape routes and hiding places. As he ran, he recorded where each hiding spot was and marked each escape route.

One home had a ball that was surrounded by two pieces of wood; seeing this brought back a memory Rico had with his young kids. Rico heard himself saying:

"Tony, what I'm about to teach you can never be told to anyone outside of our home; this training will be hard and will never end. But this training must be invisible to everyone else; what you are learning can only be used as a last resort. Do you understand me, Leon, and Tory?"

He remembered each of their first lessons: Wiohes, Cloven clan, you must respond to orders without hesitation. Tony started by killing bugs, and they graduated to Leon falling quickly and safely and Tory excellently camouflaging herself. Hand-to-hand combat was taught with Wiohes; while Tony hesitated at first, in time, he would also teach the smaller Cloven clansman. Tory took these lessons as games, learning quickly.

Tony excelled at de-escalating situations, while Leon struggled to learn these techniques.

Leon was exceptional when it came to inflicting and withstanding pain.

Rico remembers how the Cloven clan taught each other lessons without him telling them. He was amazed at how quickly Leon learned from Tory and how Tony took directions from his siblings.

As the years grew, the young ones' knowledge also grew so much that Tony couldn't teach them all they needed to learn. So, he invited friends or paid professionals to teach them all those skills they needed to be better assassins.

Along the way, the Cloven clan were all given subliminal messages that showcased how great they were and how much they were loved by their parents.

As his run continued, he laughed slightly at the memory of how both boys learned about medicines and which to use on themselves for safety and which to use on others to harm them.

He recalled how his daughter learned this but was always the cooler of the bunch. They learned about natural remedies and weapons of nature. Before he walked into his home, the rain camouflaged his tears as he remembered the game of wooden ball that turned into a painful trap his young ones had to learn how to get out of while blindfolded. Each son had to go through this a few times before getting out of the trap and graduating to a new lesson. Tory passed this painful test on her second attempt.

When he returned home, Rico remembered his late wife reminding him to pray before waking up the kids. She began her prayer by saying "Our Fadduh awt'n Hebb'n."

Rico entered his elder son Tony's room. Turning the lights

on, he told Tony to wake up and get his brother and sister up. "I'm going to the shower," Rico said as he left Tony's room.

"I see you, Dad," Tony said as he got up and woke his little brother. "Lee-Lee, come on, time for school, lil bro," Tony whispered to his little brother as he pulled his dreadlocks out of his face. Leon got up and went to his sister's room. "Time to learn, lil sis," Leon said as he entered her room. They all went to their bathrooms to get ready for school.

When the boys finished in their bathrooms, they went to the living room where Rico was already dressed in his dark blue pinstriped suit, silky black dress shirt, red and black tie, and messenger bag. Tony Cloven was dressed in dark grey pants, a midnight blue shirt, and a black vest, with a messenger bag and dreadlocks that fell just past his shoulders. Leon Cloven wore blue jeans and a light green collared dress shirt. Tory wore an olive green skirt and a dark blue collared shirt. They all had mahogany brown shoes on. Rico and Tony's shoes were Stacy Adam's leather dress shoes, while Leon's and Tory's were low-cut boots.

Rico informed his young ones that he had some new routes on their home front. They all needed to review their Koogler and learn these routes this week. The Koogler, which was a smartphone on steroids, was designed by Eliza Beth, the young Clovnes' mother, and it allowed the user to do many things as well as communicate and interface with their agency as well as each other.

Friday was a normal high school day for Tony. This day was just another middle school day for Leon as well. Tory was enrolled in a new type of school that was a combination of homeschool and private school. Rico, on the other hand, found out his assignment had been pushed up to this weekend instead of next weekend.

When the young ones got home Friday evening, Rico informed them he would be gone this weekend instead of next weekend, and his boys understood as they prepared the guest room in case there were people from their dad's office. Tory, on the other hand, was mad because this weekend was an ice cream date for the family she thought she would miss.

The young ones' weekend went well. Tony took his little siblings to the mall to watch a football game on Saturday, and on Sunday morning, they got a visitor. Tony used this time to visit his friends for the remainder of the day while Leon and Tory asked Hope, the young lady assigned to them, to watch an early movie. Hope surprised them with an ice cream date after the movie. She then stopped to pick up a gift for Tory that the men in her family had purchased before bringing them home to meet up with Tony. Hope promised to teach Tory how to use this gift.

Rico spent his weekend in Albuquerque, NM, where he assassinated three men.

The first man, Nash, was a corrupt businessman who had stolen from elderly people and pocketed their life earnings. His weakness for thick women would be his downfall. The courts had caught up to him twice before. Once, he had five years of jail time, and the second time, he was ordered to pay back every cent he stole; it took him five years to do so. Now, he was back to his old ways.

This time, within one year, he had pocketed more than ten million dollars and killed three people; this last deal, these last few letters to sign, would ensure he got away scot-free with nothing leading back to him. Unbeknownst to him, every cent he had stolen had been accounted for and traced back to his fake company.

Rico and an associate he had never met had been called to assassinate this man whom the government had been setting up for the last year.

Rico's partner would be wearing all purple; she would be size 12 and have dreadlocks that fell to the middle of her back.

She is Ms. LaVen Demur, an assassin with skills that mirror those of Rico; only she works mostly in South America. After a Koogler meeting at 0830 that lasted ten minutes, both Rico and Ms. Demur knew their roles in the assassination.

At 1000, Ms. Demur flirted with Nash as she showed him the paperwork he needed to sign. Her eyes, her lips, her body coerced him to the rooftop to sign the paperwork out of view of any cameras.

When they reached the rooftop, Ms. Demur sprayed a solution on Nash's back; when he turned to ask her what she was doing, their lips met as she rubbed in another solution on his back.

In her Brazilian accent, she told him she wanted him for one night and wanted him to carry her scent with him all day until they met again.

She went to her knees to open a giant trunk; once open, she put her body halfway in, pulling out a few items. Nash's fondness for thick women had his attention as his eyes were fixated on her appetizing curves, alluring scent, and bountiful hair as she entered the trunk again and again to retrieve different items.

"Wait here, Mr. Nash; I must run downstairs," she said, biting her lower lip while giving Nash a sexy look. "I promise to return shortly."

As she left, an image was projected on the wall in front of Nash. The image began to move as a voice told Nash of all his discretions and how he was given a chance to change. The solution Ms. Demur combined on Nash's back illuminated Rico's target, making it easier to see him in midday.

Lastly, the image told him he had been sentenced to death;

at that moment, Nash felt his body lunge forward as blood splattered against the wall in front of him. Rico had just shot him twice from the building 800 meters away. When Nash turned around, Rico shot him a third time in his chest. Nash fell to the ground; Mr. LaVen Demur walked through the door, smiling at him as he took his last breaths.

"Open your eyes, Puta, olha para est beleze, look at this beauty, and this will be the last thing your evil eyes will ever see," she said, smothering him until he died. She then placed his body in the trunk and waited until Rico joined her again.

Rico pulled the trunk from the rooftop, down a flight of stairs, into the elevator, and finally, he and Ms. Demur put the trunk in the back of an unmarked van. Ms. Demur and Rico exchanged pleasantries before going to their next assignments.

The second man Rico had to assassinate was Javier, a drug kingpin and an all-around jerk who liked molesting and raping women and men. After studying his notes and Javier's habits, Rico had learned that Javier only went out without his security on Saturdays when he visited several clubs, where no one knew his true identity.

At 2130, Rico followed him to a dance club, where he let Javier see him. Rico teased him before he left. A half-hour later, Rico got to the second club a few minutes after Javier, and again, he ensured Javier saw him. Javier attempted to get closer to Rico, but Rico accidentally on purpose missed him. After 45 minutes, Rico left this club, and he ensured Javier saw him leaving.

The last club was only a block or two away, so Rico walked it, and Javier followed him. When Rico walked into the club with a rainbow on the door, Javier was overcome with joy. Unfortunately, Javier was up to his old ways at this gay nightclub, pissing off the club patrons and disrespecting the men on the floor.

Javier finally caught up to Rico at the bar. They discussed nightlife, money, and the state of the political environment in New Mexico. Javier told Rico he wasn't gay. He just liked to party with gay men. With this, Rico excused himself from the conversation as he went to the dance floor. Rico and the other patrons enjoyed themselves on the dance floor until Javier, who was "slightly" intoxicated at this time, came to the dance floor aggressively grinding on different men, squeezing their butts, and rubbing against their dicks.

Most of the men pushed him away and attempted to avoid him. This was until Javier started to grind on Rico during a popular dance step song while everyone was dancing, not focusing on this jerk when the beat dropped.

Rico stabbed him through his right rib cage, then stabbed him twice more in his left rib cage. Javier didn't notice at first because of the crowd and his own adrenaline. As the song ended, he noticed Rico at the bar; as he took a step in Rico's direction, Rico began speaking with one of the handsome patrons at the bar.

Rico stood and rubbed the man's back as Javier fell to the floor hard. The bartender told the bouncers to get this jerk out; he had done this before, so the bouncers knew him all too well. They threw Javier out back, where one of his past molestation victims was with a group of his friends.

Rico put on a set of Koogler that resembled sunglasses as he walked out and looked at the victim, asking, "Is this the man that raped you?" The victim was in shock but confirmed by shaking his head up and down. Rico told the victim, "He is yours now; he won't fight back; oh, and they pick up the trash tomorrow."

The victim and his friends all beat Javier, robbed him, and threw him in a dumpster, where he took his last breaths.

The third man Rico must assassinate is a pastor who had been convicted nine times and fled nine states on charges of embezzlement, extortion, bankruptcy fraud, incest, rape, sodomy, manslaughter, and murder.

Rico and his employer have recently been giving the green light on Pastor Romans because there was a decision to remove just him or his entire lineage. Pastor Romans had led his latest flock astray as he gets richer, attempts to impregnate many of the church's teenage members, and had affairs with women and a man of his congregation. He is suspected of planning the murder of the man he was having an affair with because he had done this three times in the past.

Rico attended Pastor Romans' church the next morning at the 1100 service, striking up a conversation with the pastor and other members of the congregation after church services. While still amid the congregation, Rico told the pastor he had a way the church could make about $300,000 next year, and he could guarantee the first month. Telling everyone the church had been visited over the last year by a few of his investors, and they all felt that the church would use this money correctly for themselves and their community. Members of the church were excited because some of them have had conversations with Rico's investors.

At first, Pastor Roman hesitated, but then he invited Rico to his office. Using his Koogler smart device, Rico showed the pastor how everything worked and showed him testimonies from other churches they had helped in the past. Pastor Roman invited Rico to meet him for lunch at a diner on the outskirts of town.

During their meal, a male waiter took their order; he was nice, respectful, and attentive, but none of this mattered to the pastor as he told the young man, "I don't want a faggot serving me anything." Rico admonished the pastor, telling him to apologize to this young man because he hadn't done anything wrong other than be nice. Rico and the Pastor debated on how to treat members of the LGBT community. The Pastor said the bible said, and before he could finish, Rico said, "GOD doesn't make mistakes, and you will respect this young man in my presence, or I will take my money and influence elsewhere. What he did when he was in his personal time was none of your or my business." With this, the pastor angrily apologized to the young man.

The young man thanked Rico as he stood to shake the young man's hand. "C1 and C2 are delivered to you," Rico said to the young man as they parted ways. Rico then asked the pastor why he felt so strongly towards that young man. Pastor Roman replied that he just didn't like gay men. Rico got his attention and asked if it was because he secretly wanted a man; the pastor just smiled and asked how they would receive the money he promised. "Your money will be transferred to the church's account, and you don't have to insult him; just have a conversation with him, but I doubt you are his type," Rico added.

A beautiful female waitress asked the pastor if he was coming to see her at the strip club later. Rico told her he would be there, but he was sure the pastor, a man of God, was too scared to come with him. To Rico's surprise, Pastor Roman said the club she stripped at was one he frequented; she knew him; he tipped well when he laid hands on them.

A few hours later, Rico met the Pastor at the strip club where they talked about the money for the church, then some scams Pastor Roman had been president over, then they discussed what to do to these beautiful naked women as the pastor slapped a woman on her ass and tried to kiss her. In his drunken state, the pastor confessed to trying to impregnate the teens and using the church's money for his own gain.

"I keep fucking this big one, she is about 16 years old, she is so scary she isn't going to tell anyone because I make sure she always has new clothes, so she is good."

"You know Rico, I've been fucking these little girls for about five years, I got one pregnant, but she and the baby died when she went into labor early, I need a legacy, and one of these girls is going to give me one."

"Guess what, Rico, it's not just the teen girls; I'm fucking some of those married women you saw on the front row too. Did I mention I got a boyfriend, too? His wife doesn't know he is gay, but if you stick around long enough, you will see him tonight; he thinks I love him; the poor fool fell for it hook, line, and sinker."

Then he told Rico that the church would only know we had

received $60,000; the other half would go to him.

"Fuck it, I plan on taking about $30,000 of what they think we receive too."

Rico excused himself to go to the restroom and talked to the manager because this strip club happened to be on the payroll of Rico's employer. The manager and Rico ensured they had all the evidence they needed on a Koogler to convict Pastor Roman. Not only had he confessed to Rico tonight, but they also had over a year's worth of confessions of everything he had done, from extortion, incest, and even murder.

When Rico returned, he had the pastor escorted to a VIP room where he was promised to have his fantasy served. The pastor agreed, saying to Rico, "Young man, I'll talk to you later, but it's time these bitches noticed me."

As the pastor noticed the young man from the diner serving drinks, he detoured to the young man at the bar. "Hey you, I apologize for earlier, but if you meet me in the back, I'll make it up to you," he said, scanning his hand to deposit a few hundred dollars at the bar.

Reaching his VIP section, the pastor stripped down as a woman with a strap-on passed in front of him. "Come on, suck this dick," he told her. A few minutes into this fellatio act, the woman pulled away and stood up to show the pastor her strap-on.

The pastor commenced to suck on the dildo before allowing her to enter him from behind. He screamed in pleasure as he attempted to take every inch of the 10-inch dildo; his eyes watered when the woman thrust harder inside of him.

When she pulled out, the pastor forced her to the floor as he attempted to have his way with the petite woman; she begged him to stop. This only enticed the pastor. "Hey, you don't give her everything. I want some of you too," the young man from the bar whispered in the pastor's ear.

The young man rubbed the pastor's back and told him to eat her pussy first. As the pastor began his cunnilingus, he could feel the young man rubbing his neck. Then, as they practiced, the young man rammed a blade between Pastor Roman's C1 and C2 vertebrae.

Simultaneously, the young lady removed her body while forcing the pastor's face into the leather seat she was just lying on. Rico came in as the pastor was bleeding out. He began to read to him what charges he had violated and what statutes from the U.S. gave Rico the right to remove him from society.

Every confession Rico heard from the pastor, along with other confessions and evidence, was sent to the church along with the $100,000 Rico promised. The church never knew what happened to the pastor other than he ran away again, but they moved in a better direction with the money for the community.

Rico didn't get home until Monday afternoon. He sent a text to his young ones that read: "Homerun, ICU...1." Each of his young ones sent him a text that read "U.I, C...1."

.......Cloven....... □........(1).....

.........Rowe..... □.....(2).......

Hillman (Hill) Rowe kissed his wife, Seaven Rowe, on the cheek before he left for the weekend. Seaven woke up about an hour later to text Hillman to ensure he had made it to his destination. Hill told her that he was walking into his hotel room as they texted, and he would call her later before he headed out. Seven texted Hill: "Talk to you then."

When Hill opened the door to his hotel room, he could hear the shower water running, so he put his bags down on the sofa before entering the bathroom. Steam billowed out when he opened the door; he could see the figure of a woman behind the glass shower door. "Come get in, Hillman, and do my back," a female voice beckoned. Hill smiled, saying, "Give me a second," as he began to undress.

Seaven sent a text message that read: WAKE UR ASS, UPPPP!!!!!! As she pissed, standing up after wiping herself and flushing the toilet.

She went to the shower, washed her body, and shampooed and conditioned her kinky natural hair. Getting out of the shower, she stood in front of the steam-covered mirror, looking at her obscured figure. Wiping just the portions of the mirror that showed her face, she said something, but it was barely heard; then she looked on the bathroom sink to open a black box that contained a clear hearing aid.

Seaven placed the hearing aid in her ear and spoke again in a voice that was unbalanced and sounded like a child learning to speak: Invigorating thoughts of you from time to time.

Seaven smiled as she wrapped her hair before going to the kitchen in her terry cloth robe. The clear case surrounding her cell phone blinked red and blue, indicating a text was received, so Seaven picked up the phone. Her text read: Leave me alone, woman, call me when you have some downtime.

Seaven walked to her little girl's room and flicked the light off and on a few times before she entered the room, pulling the covers off her daughter. Seaven stood in front of Sierra and said: "Wake up, my dear," in her unbalanced voice.

"Momma, is today Friday?" Sierra asked her mom.

"Yes, Ci-Ci, it is. Now, get ready for school."

Sierra went to get ready in the living room while Seaven got ready in her room. When Sierra was ready, she went to the living room to find her mother watching television. Sierra tapped her mother on her right shoulder, then stood in front of her and signed: "How does this look?"

Seaven smiled and signed: "Beautiful. Now, let me do your hair."

Sierra had a regular day at school, while on the weekend, Seaven's friend Adora-Mai stopped by a few times. On Friday, they all went shopping and ate; on Saturday, they had brunch and watched a movie; and on Sunday, all three ladies went to the eight o'clock church service. After returning on Sunday, Sierra took a nap at Adora-Mai's home. While she slept, Mai and Seaven undressed as they watched television and explored Mai's bedroom.

Hill encouraged her lips to separate as she inhaled, followed by an extended exhale. She then shook her head from left to right, her eyes closing, and then gave a devilish grin. It was only then that her mind and sexy body seemed to coordinate. Hill assured her they were near the end. Her magnificent body once again called to him. Stroking her red hair, Hill whispered sweet nothings in her ear.

Helen pulled away, her red hair brushing gently against Hill's face and bald head. "Thank you, Hill, but you know it's time for you to go," Helen whispered.

Hill responded, "Just think, in about a week, you will be a lawyer, my very own sexy lawyer."

"Yeah, a lawyer who loves a married man, Hill. We must stop this before your wife or your child catches us."

"Calm down, Helen; my wife is okay as long as I don't bring anything home to her," Hill said. Helen stroked her red hair with a confused look. "Your wife doesn't care that you are fucking another woman, then comes home to fuck her? Oh, I forgot, fucking a white bitch, as the black women call me."

"Well, my dear, that's just it; she doesn't want to know what I am doing with other women; as long as I take care of home, I'm good. So, come here, baby," Helen signaled Hill to her shoulder. "So, if you are fucking me, who is your wife fucking?" Hill's eyes widened as he accidentally bit down on Helen's shoulder. An awkward silence filled the room as Hill was both stunned and infuriated at the question.

"Woman, why are you trying to ruin this? This moment we are enjoying."

"I'm sorry, baby, but I've stumbled on a picture of her, and she has beautiful dark caramel skin, a thick body, and long jet-black natural hair; I mean, a black woman with that much hair has to be mixed with something, and you know men are probably constantly putting in their application, especially after they find out she is in an open relationship."

"Helen, what do you want from me? I told you what this was when we began this years ago. I know when you pass the bar, we will be no more, so, for now, let us enjoy…as long as we can."

"Hill, I understand what you are saying. I just don't want any of this to come to bite me in the butt. You paid my way through college, and my parents never even asked me where the money came from. You even paid for my divorce from Luke. You have done all this for a future lawyer who, if not careful, could get disbarred. I thought marrying Luke would curve my appetite for you, but it only intensified when I was witness to his deplorable habits and his unrelenting attitude toward anyone who didn't look like him."

"Speaking of Luke, he is going to have Billy at the end of next week. My brothers have agreed to talk to him about our move to Savannah. I'm meeting all of them at that park that's off 3rd and Ponce to pick up Billy at the end of Luke's visit."

Hill and Helen's weekend went on without any hiccups and with one promise: Hill had agreed to leave his wife.

…..Rowe……□……….(2)……....

………Who is who……□……..(3)…..

The next day, at the beginning of the school day, Tony met Mike and Tamiko, who were both in 9th grade. He asked, "Where is your brother? He needs to hurry up before we are late for class," Tony urged.

At that moment, Ken jumped from behind a tree, attempting to scare Tony. Mike and Tamiko laughed as their brother scared his best friend. "Boy, you better stop; I might have to hit you next time," Tony warned.

"Aw, you gonna hit a blind guy?" Ken retorted.

"Tony says you have low vision," Mike chimed in.

Tony swung at Ken; Ken deflected the punch and followed with a headlock. Tony shouted to Mike and Tamiko, "Oh, y'all just gonna let him do me like this."

They all play-fought for a minute until the school bell rang. Ken stopped just before the bell rang. "Mike and Miko, get to class. I'll see you all after school," Ken said in a commanding voice.

Mike and Miko hugged their brother and Tony, then headed to class. Tony asked, "Hey, Ken, you ready for this day?"

Ken replied, "I see you, man," as he reached for Tony's left elbow.

While most of their classes were in different halls, Tony

made sure to get Ken to the hall his class was in before going to his class.

Their favorite class was the last class of the day, weight training. Both young men enjoyed this class because it gave them a chance to blow off some steam; plus, this was the room where they first met three years earlier.

Ken had been lured there by a group of boys who were going to take his money and beat him because he was blind, and they thought he wouldn't defend himself.

Tony was looking for an answer to one of Leon's riddles on his first day at his new school when he happened upon the scene. Ken held his own until he was forced to the ground.

Tony jumped in as Ken hit the ground. Ken could hear the boys attempting to hit Tony, so when he got to his feet, he told Tony to send them his way.

The two boys worked together to fight off six other boys until the coaches and teachers ran in to break things up. Five of the six boys were sent to the hospital, while the sixth was found hiding.

The bullies' parents all wanted to press charges against the black boys who had brutalized their sons and sued the school. They all came together to show that their sons were Christian members of clubs in the school and would be productive members of society.

They planned to demonstrate that the two black kids were thugs and menaces to the community and should be expelled. Furthermore, they all sought compensation from the school for their pain, suffering, and hospital bills.

Their story gained national attention, from jury selection to the verdict. All the bullies shared a group of three lawyers, and each had two witnesses to testify on their behalf to show how harmless they were.

Their lawyers could only present statistics to argue why young black men were thugs and high school dropouts.

Lastly, their lawyer came up with a scenario as to how things could have happened. When the bully lawyers finished, the nation thought they had won the case, and certain segments of society were celebrating.

Tony and Ken's three lawyers first brought in 24 witnesses to testify on behalf of Ken or how they were bullied by each of the six bullies. Secondly, they brought out all six bullies' police records, school attendance, and grades.

Lastly, Ken and Tony's lawyers showed a video of how the boys lured Ken into the weight room, how they took his money, and then how they attempted to beat him until Tony showed up. This video then showed how brutally Tony and Ken beat the boys with only their fists when they all used weapons on him and Ken.

Tony and Ken's lawyers then did something unexpected; they counter-sued for triple what the lawsuit was against them. They also brought the parents' business into play, showing how each business was illegally run, financial missteps, money laundering, drugs, and illegal firearm sales.

Lastly, their lawyers got each boy to confess that he had a hand in the beating or had them tell on another boy. This provoked the judge and jury to hand down punishment to all the bullies. Although the punishments were not stiff, they did stick, and all eventually moved to different towns or states.

A few years later, like most days, Ken and Tony waited for Mike and Miko but talked about each other with friends.

"Leather suspenders: what black man does this, Ken?" Tony asked. "Dreadlocks, what black woman? Oops, I mean, man wants that nest; damn, I mean mess on their head."

They were joined by a multicultural group of friends. Chris, the rich, humble kid, was a white guy with the surfer look. Rose was a young lady born in India who loved music but was a hip-hop head and a DJ. Drea, a young black woman who walked with a cane because of multiple sclerosis, was the smartest one in the group. Rich, the undeniable ladies' man, was a tall, muscular, pretty boy, and Basilio, a.k.a Solo, was a Puerto Rican college-bound football player.

Over the past three years, they had become close, even referring to each other as family. Many nights were spent at Tony's house because his dad had the most relaxed rules. Plus, all the parents had benefited from Tony's dad's company, which built homes, did interior decorating, and all types of landscaping work, from cutting grass to building extra homes onto existing homes.

Rico's prices were hard to beat, especially if you were willing to work on your own projects.

The gang often did homework at Tony's house or played some type of game, but the hardest game for them was football. Leon would observe their interactions and absorb everything he saw and heard from his older brother and his friends. Tory's eyes would light up when the teens were outside playing any game. Yet there was one game that Leon questioned them about: "How can all of you play football if Ken can't see and Drea can't walk?"

So, one day, Ken told Leon to stand in one spot on the field. Tory tagged along, too, but she was curious and quiet. He then saw Ken quarterback for both three-on-three teams. Drea, Chris, and Solo were on one team that usually did long passes, while Rose, Tony, and Rich were on the other team who usually ran short passes. Leon and Tory were instructed to close their eyes at the snap of each play.

At first, Leon heard a lot of hollering and talking. After the third play, he could hear a clicking sound that was in a pattern. Tory shouted, "Lee-lee, the click sounds; listen for the clicks." When he opened his eyes, he saw Ken throw the ball in the general area of the player, making a specific clicking noise. Drea would either use her upper body strength to help protect Ken when her team had the ball, or she would distract players from catching the ball.

Leon saw them as family and was sad when they were angry with one another. Tory was usually around to bring them back together. While the group cared for each other, there were always questions they wanted to know about each other, so over the years, everyone would learn the answers to these questions, except for one: Why does Tony have burn scars on his back?

Rich, in particular, had always wanted to know about Tony's scars, so one Thursday night, he got up the nerve to ask Tony. He asked the second in command of their group, Ken, first because he didn't want to disrespect their leader, Tony. Tony didn't want to answer the question, but he decided after a few days of peer pressure from Ken to tell all his friends about the bullet wound in his shoulder and the burned skin on his back. It took Tony roughly three hours to tell his friends a story they would never forget.

He started the story with, "My baby sister was with Hope, and my little brother, Lee-Lee, for the past two nights, filled the bathtub with cold water and submerged bath towels in the water. The weird thing was he would only use Red, Blue, and Black towels. My mother's favorite color was Red, my dad's favorite color was Blue, and my favorite color is..."

Before he could finish, his friends all said, "Black."

"My mother caught him the first night after all the towels were submerged. As she walked into the bathroom, he was crying when he threw the red towel at her. She panicked and asked him what was wrong and why he was crying. He said, 'Mommy, no one is moving, and it's hot, and she told me to protect you, I must put wet towels on you.'"

This terrified our mother, so she told our dad, who sat Leon down and asked him about what happened. Leon didn't remember why the water was running, but he did remember everyone's favorite color.

"The second night, I caught him just as he was putting the towels in the water. He shouted as loud as he could, 'TONY, GET DOWN! I PROTECT YOU!!!!' Before he ran and jumped on my back and squeezed. My dad had to pull him off my back because he was squeezing me so hard it was hurting.

My parents talked to him again and asked him what was wrong. He told them something different than he told them

Thursday night: 'I have to protect momma because it's hot; in my dream, mommy, you told me it will get hot, and I have to put these water towels on top of y'all.'

On Friday, my dad caught him and told him to go to bed, but this time, he didn't fight back or cry. On Saturday, he begged everyone to sleep downstairs in the living room, and we all did for a little while. My dad eventually told us to go to bed. My dad woke up a few minutes later to see Leon in the tub filling it up again. My dad says he doesn't know why, but he submerged the towels as my little brother asked.

When I woke up, my back was burning, but when I opened my eyes, there was someone in front of me, so I hit him and stood up, then I saw a police officer looking at me in horror; I heard a boom then my shoulder started burning. Lee reached me when I hit the ground and placed a cold towel on my head and shoulder before heading back to our burning house. I passed out again and didn't remember anything after this, but I was told this is what happened next."

Someone started a fire at the empty house next door to ours. This fire eventually attacked our house. The police were called by one of our neighbors who had not been sleeping well all week. When the fire got to our house, the smoke from the fire knocked out my mother, my father, and me, but Lee had a small, wet black towel that was identical to my big black towel on his face.

He used his wagon to get me out, but not before my back was set ablaze. He pulled me out the front door as a crowd of people looked on in amazement. He placed a wet rag on my back before dumping me on the lawn. The police had arrived, and two of them were trying to help. I hit the first one, and the second one shot me without hesitation.

That sound must have scared Leon because they said he turned and ran as fast as he could to place his rag on me before I passed out after the cop shot me. He then got my dad, who was on the couch, placing one big wet blue towel over his face, chest, and thighs. He pulled my dad out, dumped him on the lawn, and before he could go back in, was stopped by the police.

He somehow got one of their guns free and shot in the air, distracting everyone. He then ran upstairs to get our mother.

This is where it got crazy because the cops and paramedics said our mother had already died from smoke inhalation, the same thing that almost got my dad and me when Lee got to her bedroom and pulled her off the bed and into his wagon. He pulled her and the wagon downstairs before pulling her outside and hitting her chest.

But Leon said our mother was waiting for him at the top of the stairs, lying on her stomach, with her red towel already on her head. He said she told him to help her downstairs so she could get in his wagon. Her last words, according to Leon, were: "Tell Rico our little ones are welcomed; I love you all." Then she kissed him.

According to witnesses, when Lee came through the door, he was laying on top of our mother, and as soon as the wagon hit the lawn, he began hitting or rather pushing her stomach. He was telling the paramedics this would wake her up; this would wake Mommy up as they peeled him off her to do CPR like they were doing for us. Unfortunately, she was already gone, but the paramedics noticed three things about her.

The first was that her clothes were not burned like my dad's and mine. Secondly, my mother had a smile on her face when they got to her, and the last thing was that the back of her hands and arms were burned badly, as though she was protecting something on her chest.

The cops had a hard time pulling Leon away from our mother; he was hitting, kicking, screaming, biting, and fighting. The cops were getting angry and attempting to put him in handcuffs until an old lady from the crowd yelled as loud as she could: "STOP!!!" as she ran as quickly as she could to them.

Leon fought harder when he saw the paramedic place a sheet over our mother's head. He screamed a blood-curling scream: "NOOOO!!!, MOMMY DOESN'T LIKE THAT!!!!, HER CAN'T SEE ME, HER CAN'T SEE ME!!!!"

The old woman finally reached them, saying, "I called y'all; let that child go."

"Ma'am, get out of here; we got this," one of the Policemen screamed at her.

The old woman would not move but argued with the cops. One of the cops pulled a gun on her, but she stood her ground, saying, "Give him to me." She looked at Leon and said something my mother often said to us: "Come, my child."

Leon stopped his fighting; the cops were so amazed they stopped what they were doing, too.

The woman came to one knee and said again, "Come, my child." Leon, with tears in his eyes, ran to her and hugged her tight, shouting, "MOMMY CAN'T SEE ME! We have to get the cover off her."

A young pregnant mother ran and removed the cover from her mother's face and began to rub her own face.

Leon, dragging the old lady by her hand, ran to his mother's side. The crowd wouldn't allow the paramedics to move her body into the ambulance until Leon got to her.

When Lee got to our mother, he asked everyone to hold hands; when they did so, Lee said, "Mommy, everyone helps me today; see, Mommy, I did what you said; I asked for help..." He rubbed the side of her face as he said, "Mommy… I see you." Only then would he allow the sheet to go over her face.

He turned to the old lady and said, "My mommy is not here anymore, ma'am." With tears in her eyes, she asked, "Where is your mommy's child?"

He looked around the crowd, searching for her, then he looked up. He pulled the old lady close; she knelt. Leon rubbed the left side of her face and turned her face toward the rising sun. "Mommy is there," he said as he pointed toward the beautiful sky.

Every witness said that at that moment, a rush of air began unusually hot, then warm, turned cooled, then as cold as snow when it rushed past them, and this wind was blowing for about 60 seconds.

That was in the summer when Leon was only about eight or nine years old; my sister was even younger, and we moved here that September. I graduate this year, and my little brother is in the 9th grade; my sister has been placed in seventh grade; even though it happened all those years ago, we don't talk about it much. When we do, our father tells us more about our mother, things we didn't know about her, facts that are amazing and far-fetched, I think, but these make us miss her more because we have so many questions to ask her.

"Did you all know my mother was Black, but her grandmother was Native American?" I tell you all this because when most people see her picture and painting around our home, they think she is a model; one painting in particular, most people think this is a picture. It was a painting my dad and us little ones painted of her a year before she died.

……Who is who........ □........(3)....
…… Invigorating thoughts of you........ □........(4).....

The day had finally come again when Seaven would take her daughter to a park for a mother/daughter lunch date.

As soon as she could, Sierra asked her mother if she could go play on the playground.

Instead of simply saying yes, Seaven signed to her daughter, "Yes, child, but be careful. Get my attention if you need me."

Sierra signed back, "Yes, ma'am," just as she sprinted toward the playground area.

Rico, Leon, and Tory happened to be eating at a bench next to Seaven and Sierra that led to the play area and witnessed the conversation between Seaven and Sierra.

"Dad, what are they saying? Do you know sign language?" Leon asked, puzzled.

"I do know, Lee," his dad responded. "But why don't you go ask the little girl what was said, lil' man."

"O.k., I'll be back, daddy," Leon said as he sprinted to the playground area.

Tory asked, "Daddy, can only deaf people learn sign language?"

"Everyone can learn," Rico responded. "And why do you ask?"

"I want to learn sign language and remix it for our family."

"Okay, I see you," her dad said with a smile, "we will begin your lessons soon."

Rico got Seaven's attention after she sat down with her and her daughter's snacks.

Seaven smiled because she recognized this man smiling at her.

She rushed over to hug him.

Rico stood, they embraced, and Seaven whispered, "This cannot be."

They embraced for a moment or two longer.

Rico could only say, "Wow, wow, wow."

He then requested Seaven to put in her hearing aid by tapping his right ear with his left index finger, making a fist, then opening his hand, allowing his fingers to spread.

Seaven smiled, put in her hearing aid, and before she could realize what she had done, she began to sign.

Rico signed back, but he told her to speak because he loved the sound of her voice.

The first words she heard from his mouth were, "Invigorating thoughts of you from time to time. You are magnificent, powerful, and intriguing, ummm, beautiful... Now speak to me."

Tory gazed at her father in amazement and joy.

Leon learned that Sierra's mom was legally deaf but could hear with a hearing aid that she hated to wear in public.

While climbing in the play area, there was a bully who was pushing down and hitting other kids, but Sierra and Leon had both, by chance, missed him because of the conversation they were having.

Even though there were other kids in the play area, Sierra's focus was on Leon and vice versa.

She explained what deaf meant to Leon, but he also wanted

to learn some sign language because his dad knew some sign language.

Leon told Sierra he would be right back as he ran to his dad to get more to drink.

He ran to Rico, saying, "Dad, I can sign. Watch!" He showed his dad the letters A, B, C, and drank his juice.

"Lee, don't be rude. Say hello, son," Rico told his son.

"Oh, hello, Si… Sa… umm, Seaven," said Sierra.

Leon smiled ear to ear, saying, "I liked your voice, Sierra's mom," as he ran back to the play area.

"Ouch! No! Get off me!" Sierra screamed as the bully pushed his knee into her back.

All the parents looked on in horror as Seaven screamed, "My bab! My bab! Do somethin'!"

Leon heard Sierra's screams as he climbed to the top of the play area where Sierra was being held.

Leon approached the bully and without any hesitation hit the bully in his ear, causing him to release Sierra and fall.

Leon wrapped his arms around Sierra as they fell down a slide.

As they reached the bottom, both of their parents were there, but Rico caught them before they hit the ground.

The people in the park erupted with cheers as Rico held the kids.

But the cheers were short-lived as the bully's dad rushed to his child who had chosen a different route to get off the play area, running to his father crying.

The little nigger boy daddy and the nigger boy screamed as loud as he could to his dad and his friends who were sitting at one of the tables further out from the playground area.

"Point 'em out, Billy. Which one done did it?" Billy's dad said as they rushed over to Rico and company.

Everyone in earshot has now stopped as they watch all the action in the playground area. "Hey boy, did you hit my child?" Billy's dad shouted to Leon.

"Whoa, step back. That's my child, and you will not speak to him," Rico yelled back in a tone that disturbed the bully's dad.

"Well, that lil' nigglet hit my child, and either you or him can take this ass whopping, boy," Rico said, facing Seaven. Seaven without hesitation got all the kids out, hers and those that didn't belong to her. Rico's two kids somehow got away and stood on either side of their dad.

The other parents, all mothers, rushed to get their kids and thanked Sierra as they exited the play area. Rico stood tall against this idiot and his two buddies. Staring at the bully's dad directly in his eyes, Rico said calmly with the blink of his eyes. Rico's face has changed from welcoming to menacing. "Hit dat nigger daddy, the lil nigger boy hit me he deserves it, daddy."

"Come on, Luke you saw for yourself Billy was hurting that little girl, yall get off me, you nigger lovers," Luke said, pushing them away.

"Well, go ahead Mike, tell me why we not supposed to call them niggers, tell me Larry again why they equal to us, you fucking nigger lovers, get out of er . I hate yall just as much as I hate him now. You tell em dad, nigger lovers, all of em. " Mike and Larry raised their hands and turned their backs to Luke.

Mike said, "Sir, we have called the police, and we will give a statement about this asshole," Larry chimed in, "What your son did, needed to be done." Rico looked relieved and puzzled as he told them "Thank yall, they all agree let's get out of here."

Before Rico could exit the play area, Luke grabbed and punched him, but just as he hit Rico, he felt his left leg give out and experienced pain in his right side. Rico staggered into Larry's arms just as Luke grabbed his privates, and his face turned red. Mike, Larry, and Rico looked at one another in disbelief as Luke continued to fall hard to the ground. Standing before him were Leon and Tory, who had now turned their attention to Billy.

Seaven rushed past the stunned men, picked up Leon, then Tory, and placed them on top of a bench. Leon was hyperventilating as tears ran down his face.

"That man, that man hit my daddy," Tory's eyes calmly looked into Seaven's eyes. She pointed at her eye, made a fist with both hands, lowered her chin as she got into a fighting position. Her calm eyes now left Seaven's eyes and glared in Billy's direction.

In her unbalanced voice, Seaven called out, "LEON." Everyone came to a standstill as her voice echoed throughout. She began to sign, and as she did so, Sierra spoke the words she signed. Sierra's voice was now calm and echoed as she spoke: "Little prince, no more, no more violence this day. Thank you for your bravery, but now, little prince…."

Seaven looked out to the crowd with tears in her eyes, then turned back to Leon as she continued to speak: "Now, little prince… you sleep." With her fingers outstretched and spread, Seaven started at Leon's forehead and slowly traced his face with her fingers. When she reached his chin, the young boy's little body went limp, falling into her arms, his eyes closed and his breathing returning to normal as she laid him in the seating area of the bench.

Seaven raised her hands so that Tory could see her palms as she spoke, "Princess of Rico Cloven." Tory's shoulders rose just as she was about to attack Billy when Seaven shouted, "Come, my child." Tory snapped out of her trance, her fist dropped, her mouth opened, and her eyes slowly left Billy and came back to Seaven.

The moment Seaven's and Tory's eyes met, Seaven, with a forceful breath from her diaphragm, said, "REST!!!" Tory's little body, like her brother's, fell into Seaven's arms. Tory was so lightweight that Seaven stood with her.

Seaven held the little body like a baby about to be burped when she sat on the bench.

Mike rushed to get the little boy out of his seat and took him to his father.

She told him, "Thank you, he was heavier than I thought."

Rico told Larry, "Thank you, man, for the catch and for trying to help your friend, not hate."

Rico wanted to say more, but he, like everyone else, noticed how lovingly Mike was holding Leon.

Larry told them how Mike's son, Lee, was taken away from him at that age; Lee now played with the Angels.

Rico looked at this white man holding his black child and wondered how anyone could hate when there was so much pain and so much love in this world.

"Daddy loves his Lee-Lee," Mike said with tears in his eyes.

Rico rubbed Mike's back, saying, "Man, I'm sorry for your loss."

Mike looked Rico in his eyes, saying, "Sir, hold him close. There's something about your son," as he attempted to hand him to Rico.

"Mike, you can hold my Leon a bit longer."

"Lee… Leon… I love that name, sir," Mike told Rico.

When Rico looked up, he could see the police talking to the people in the park.

"Guys, the Police are here," Rico said.

Mike instinctively pulled Leon closer to him.

The policewoman asked Rico what happened, and before he could start his story, he saw 4 or 5 more police cars pull up and an ambulance.

"Mr. Rico, can you tell us what happened to Luke over there?"

Rico told the police how they heard the blood-curdling screams of Sierra, how Leon hit Billy, Luke's racial slurs toward him, Mike, and Larry, how Larry and Mike attempted to calm things down, how Luke hit him, and how his son and daughter hurt Luke and kicked him in his privates…

Then, he attempted to tell the policewoman what Seaven had done.

Larry told the same story but had a hard time telling what Seaven had done.

The policemen asked Rico about the whereabouts of his child. Rico pointed to Mike, who was holding a sleeping Leon, then to Seaven, holding a sleeping Tory. At that point, Billy's mom came in to comfort her child.

The police asked her story, which was totally different from anyone else's. She was confused as to why the police didn't believe her. She said, "I was telling y'all what Luke said happened."

Larry said, "Helen, he was lying, and you needed to reconsider his visitation rights."

Helen's eyes got big as she looked at her child, saying, "Tell me what happened, Billy."

Billy tried to lie, so Helen asked where the mother of the

little girl was, who Billy said called him the N-word. Seaven stood up and walked toward Helen with her hand outstretched to shake her hand.

Helen's mouth dropped as she came to her feet to shake Seaven's hand. Helen and Seaven went to a different bench to talk. Larry sat next to Billy as the women talked. Before they began talking, Seaven told Helen that she was legally deaf but had a hearing aid.

The women spoke for a few minutes, then Helen approached the policewoman, questioning Luke. Helen informed her that she wanted Luke arrested for child endangerment and abuse.

"Child endangerment and abuse," the policewoman questioned.

"Billy, come to mommy," Helen said to her child. She raised the little boy's shirt to show the imprint of the belt buckle that Luke was wearing.

Larry raised up, his red hair now matching his red face when he saw his nephew's back. Larry rushed over, hitting Luke in the jaw, but the policewoman jumped on top of Luke to protect him from Larry. More policewomen came in to break up the fight. When they were told what happened, they let Larry go.

Larry angrily rushed to Luke again, saying, "He ain't worth

it, he ain't worth it."

"Ma'am, could you please get this," Luke looked at Billy as Helen continued, "this sorry excuse for a man out of here, please.

Policemen were questioning other patrons at the park as Luke was carried out to one of the awaiting police cars. Larry hugged his nephew, saying, "I'm sorry, Billy, I didn't know, I didn't know. Sis, I'm sorry, I didn't know he hurt my nephew and was a racist piece of shit."

Helen gave Larry a business card that read, "Helen Gerald, Attorney at Law." Larry said, "You passed it. You passed the bar." He hugged his sister to congratulate her. Larry told Mike, Rico, and Seaven that his sister had been studying and doing everything in her power over the last few years to become a lawyer. She was congratulated by everyone.

"This joyous occasion is bittersweet because I now know how my son was being influenced by his deadbeat dad who I wanted to give him one more chance with his son," Helen confessed.

"Ms. Seaven, I apologize from the bottom of my heart," she paused, "for what happened today, and Billy wants to tell you something."

Billy came with his hand in-between his legs and said, "I'm sorry for hurting the little girl, and I want to take away everything I said." Seaven called Sierra over as Billy talked; Billy shook Sierra's hand. Seaven began to sign as Sierra commentated, "Young man, do you know what the word 'nigger' means?"

Billy said, "Luke told me to call black people that." Billy looked up to see Seaven sign more.

"No, young man, it means ignorant, and it was not a nice word, it was worse than a curse word." Billy smiled with amazement in his eyes and said, "Mommy, she was speaking with her hands."

Sierra grabbed Billy's hands and showed him how to sign, "I am sorry." Billy then signed, "I am sorry," to his mother, to Seaven, to his uncle Larry, then he went to Mike, who was still holding a sleeping Leon, and signed, "I am sorry," to him and Rico. Rico signed, "Apology accepted," to everyone's amazement.

Helen put her thumb to her chin, looking up to the left, and asked, "How did he go to sleep again?" Larry struggled to find the words, but he told his sister what he witnessed. Rico said, "I've seen her stop a bull in his tracks, so my young one was no match for whatever magic she possessed."

Seaven, in her unbalanced voice, said, "When God took my hearing, he gave me the power of peace. I wish I knew how it worked, but it did." Helen, still in amazement, said, "You caressed the little prince's face, and now he sleeps," something like that,

Seaven said, laughing.

Leon woke up momentarily, and Mike gasped for air. Leon looked around for his daddy. Rico smiled at his son. Leon looked back at Mike with a smile on his face, putting his little arm around Mike's neck; then he fell back to sleep. Mike couldn't help but allow tears to roll down his face as he smiled. Helen could only say, "Thank you, thank you, thank you, my big brother needed this.

The Police continued their investigation as Leon was handed back to Rico. The Gerald family got ready to leave, but not before Helen asked her questions.

Helen asked with a smirk, "So, how long have you two been together?" Rico responded, "We were not together; she was a happily married woman." Helen rolled her eyes as Rico continued, "But my son helped her daughter today."

Seaven asked, "Where is your husband, ma'am?" Her brothers laughed, but Helen looked Seaven in her eyes with a nasty smirk, saying, "I'm not married, but my man is working right now. Let's go, guys," Helen said with a smirk.

"What was her problem?" Rico asked. "I didn't know, but that was weird. Is she bipolar or something?" Seaven said, laughing.

As they left, Rico walked Seaven and Sierra to their vehicle. He asked Seaven a burning question. "Seaven, I had to know, is that

Leon's sister?" Before she could answer, her phone rang; she picked up and said, "Where are you?"

"Rico, I have to go, and I knew she was not because we had a DNA test done. Seaven, does she have a cluster of three moles above her private area?" Rico asked. Looking past Rico, Seaven's eyes widened, then she said, "Oh my God, Rico, I have to go."

……. Invigorating thoughts of you…….. □……..(4)…..

……This black man…….. □……(5)……

After Helen put Billy in his seat, she kissed her brothers as they went their separate ways. But as soon as she got in her car, she called Hill to tell him that his wife was at the park and that she was with a man and his son.

"Hill, she looked at him like every word he spoke sent chills down her spine," Helen said. Hill asked, "What was his name, and please tell me he wasn't black."

"I don't understand, Hill, you're black, why don't you like other black people?" Helen asked. "Was he black?" Hill said as his voice rose. Helen apologetically said, "Yes, he is a black man."

"This bitch told me she wasn't going to mess with another man; she promised me that!" Hill shouted as he questioned Helen more about what she saw. Helen answered all his questions as she drove home, but once she got to her garage, she asked, "Hill, what are you going to do about this? Can you divorce her now?"

"I will divorce her, and if he goes missing or if he happens to lose his life, that will be justified," Hill said sharply. "As you know, I will be leaving for Iraq in a few days. While I'm gone, someone will take care of him for me."

Helen was ecstatic to hear that Hill would finally leave his wife for her.

……This black man……. ☐*……(5)……*

…Adora's………. ☐*……(6)…….*

When Rico was out of view, Seaven sent a text message that read: "How long were you watching?" She then instructed Sierra to put on her headphones and watch a movie on her DVD player. Within three minutes, the car phone rang. Seaven pressed the button to answer the phone. When the phone picked up, she asked, "How long were you watching us?"

There was silence for a second. Then a female voice answered: "From the time that man picked up the little boy and Sierra."

"If that is the case, why didn't you approach me, Adora-Mai?" Seaven questioned.

Adora responded with a low voice, "Seaven, who is that man? I've never seen you look at Hill like that. Shit, you don't even look at me like that; you were attentive to every word that came out of his mouth, and you touched that man every chance you got. Seaven, baby, who is this man?"

"He is someone important to me, but it has been years since I've seen him," Seaven said as her voice quivered. "Meet me in the park for brunch tomorrow, Mai. I will tell you about him then."

Mai agreed as she told Seaven she loved her. "I'm down the street from my house, Mai. I must go," Seaven said as she made kissing sounds and pressed the button to hang up the phone.

When Seaven walked into her home, Hill gave her the cold shoulder and silent treatment. Seaven prepared Sierra's bath and told her husband about what happened. She explained that Rico was an old friend from high school and how his kids defended their daughter. She explained that a woman named Helen was the bully's mom, and that the woman gave her bad vibes.

Hill barely listened and asked how Sierra was doing before he went to bed. Sierra was put to bed in the guest room, where she shared a bed with Seaven for the night.

Hill left early the next morning while Seaven and her daughter met Adora-Mai at the park. The two women hugged before

Sierra was sent to play. Mai asked, "So, who is this Rico?"

Seaven explained that in school, because of her hearing impairment, light skin complexion, and racial background of French Creole, Native, and Black American, she didn't have too many friends until she met Rico. "He treated me like a queen, like I belonged to him, and I loved it, but he came in second when I met Hillman. The Hillman family had money, he played football, and I thought he wanted me too. Rico has never hurt me; he actually learned to sign because of me. I thought Rico had something up his sleeve because I never experienced a man treating a woman like he treated me. To make a long story short, I chose Hillman over Rico, but not before Rico gave me my first orgasm. He and I had an affair about 10 years ago, and now he thinks Sierra is his."

Mai could only smile as she rubbed Seaven's hair. "I was picked on too in school," Mai said. "There was a boy who didn't mind because I'm Japanese and Afro-Cuban; he loved me because of how we understood each other. I lost him because I chose my first girlfriend over him."

The ladies spoke and laughed for a few hours before they went their separate ways, but not before exchanging passionate kisses and a hug.

...Adora's...........□......(6)......

…who in danger…..…… □.......(7)......

Rico stopped by Ken's home to pick up Tony before heading home. "Dad, what took you and Lee so long? I had time to finish all my homework, see my girl on her phone, and play video games for a while. Oh, is that it?" Tony explained, laughing.

"Your little brother and sister got into a fight today; he hit a little boy, stabbed the boy's daddy, your sister hurt this idiot, too, and attempted to make sure the man didn't have any more kids," Rico explained.

Tony chimed in, "Did he cry again, dad?" Rico said, "Did you not hear anything I just said, Tony?"

"Yes, sir, but he would only do that if someone else was in danger… am I correct? Was someone in danger?" Tony said with a smirk on his face.

Rico said, "Well, damn… I thought it was just the little girl, but they thought I was in danger, that's why they hurt that man so bad."

"Whoa, dad, you were in danger? Who was it? Where are they, dad? Stop the car!" Tony said excitedly.

"Tony, no, no more. You have a few more months before college. No more fighting for you, well, competition only, you understand, young man?" Tony turned his head away.

"Wait… you said Tory was in this… is the man alive?" Rico smiled and said, "Tory allowed him to breathe, this time…"

Tony smiled, looking out his window. His dreadlocks fell onto his chest as he answered the question with an emphatic, "Yes, sir."

As they reached their home, Tony told Rico, "Dad, Lee-Lee is still asleep. I'll put him in bed."

"Thank you, Tony, but put him in my bed instead, please. Make sure Tory gets in bed too," Rico instructed.

"Cool, man. Oh, dad, by the way, tattoos, yea or nah?" Tony asked.

Rico looked at his handsome son with a wide smile, widening his eyes, saying, "Naaaaaaahhhhhh, you already know, shawty," Rico said, laughing.

"I had to try, dad," Tony said as he got his little brother from the garage to his dad's bed.

Now, as if rehearsed a million times, Tony went to his room, removing all his clothes, and yelled out, "Dad, I'm in the shower!" Rico responded, "Good to go, I'm stationary, I see you." Tony yelled, "I see you, dad!" as he closed his door.

Rico turned on the fireplace, got a thick blanket from the hall closet, then placed it at a 45-degree angle from the fireplace. He went to the kitchen and warmed up some leftover lasagna, Texas bread, green beans, and a large cinnamon roll. He placed all this in the oven, and once it was finished, he placed it all on a tray that he eventually placed in front of the thick blanket next to the fireplace. On a separate tray, he placed three pills next to a small glass of water, a medium glass of orange juice, and napkin and utensils. Rico sat down to watch SportsCenter.

A few minutes later, Tony walked in with his towels wrapped around his hair and his waist. Rico could see the bullet wound in his son's shoulder and the burn marks on his back. Tony had the body of an athlete, so he healed very well.

Rico told his son, "Daddy has to go shit, shower, shave; be back in a few. Listen for Leon and Tory." Rico kissed Leon on his forehead as he went to the bathroom in his bedroom. "I see you, dad," Tony responded, "I see you, son."

While watching television and eating, Tony suddenly stopped and popped up, throwing his book bag off the table before he ran to his dad's room to retrieve a box of pens, pencils, and colored pencils. He then grabbed a notebook and a large paper easel, placing all this on the table in front of the couch. Tony's phone rang, and without looking at the caller ID, he answered and told the person on the other end to "hold on, please." He went to the office to get his dad's glasses and recorder. Tony got back on the phone but hung up. About 15 minutes passed when Rico walked back to the living room in his bathrobe.

Tony and Rico discussed Tony's day, their upcoming college visit, and Tony's year in assassin school. As the conversation ended, Rico put on his glasses and began to write and draw almost in sequence.

Leon walked into the living room and spoke rather softly, "Hey, dad," rubbing his eyes, but the moment he saw Tony, his face lit up. He yelled, "Brother, Brother T, I miss yooouuu."

"Lil Dude, I just saw you this morning before school, but guess what, I miss you tooooooooo," Tony responded. They all shared a good laugh. Tony had saved a little bite of food for Leon and Tory. Leon only ate the bread, waiting for his sister to eat the rest, and then he sat in his brother's lap. Tony talked with his little brother about a book they were reading together. Rico looked over from his table 15 minutes later to see Tory eating the rest of the food as Leon had fallen asleep again. Rico picked him up and took him to his room; Tory jumped on his back and jumped off at her room.

Leon's room looked like any other 12-year-old's room, with the exception of the fighting gear and the three-foot by three-foot painting of his mother holding him with a poem entitled "Greatest" below it. Tory's room, full of purple and black, looked like any other little girl's room with the exception of fighting gear, a .45, and a picture of their mother. Tory was sitting in her mother's lap, looking up lovingly into her mother's face; the poem "Greatest" was below this picture as well.

Tony and Rico spoke some more as Tony watched television and Rico continued to write and draw. After about 45 minutes, Rico looked over to see Tony laid out on his blanket. Rico went over to get his son up so he could go to bed. Rico picked the young man up; Tony's eyes opened as he mumbled, "You're too old to carry me, shawty." Rico dropped him on his bed and covered him with a thick blanket that had the Marine Corps emblem on it. Tony's room was like any other 15-year-old's room with the exception of musical instruments, sound machines, fighting gear, and a three-foot by three-foot painting of his mother holding him with a poem entitled "Greatest" watermarked behind the picture.

Rico walked out of his room, knelt in the hallway that separated the kids' rooms, and began to pray aloud:

Our mother who are in heaven.

Bless these who have come before and those who will come after me.

Look over Tony, Bless his mind, strengthen his body and calm him to his soul.

Bestow onto him all the wisdom I cannot give and show him the love he so desperately needs from his mother. Were ever he plants himself allow his roots to spread long and thick like the mighty redwood tree.

Look over Leon, bestow your grace upon his gift and never allow him to suffer because of his gift.

Bless this child lord and allow him to love others not just his siblings and me.

Look over Tory, allow this girl to grow into the woman her mother wanted her to be.

Strengthen her mind, and allow her to see others for who they truly are.

Now lord I ask you to order my steps in your name.

Any hatred, any pain within allow it to flee from me.

Amen, times 3.

…who in danger…........☐……(7)……

……Ribs were chosen……..☐……(8)……

"Remember, Ci-Ci, you are not just a daughter, but a strong woman in the making," Hill continued, his voice filled with emotion. "You have the power to change the world, to uplift and inspire those around you. And no matter where life takes you, always remember your worth and your strength."

Ci-Ci listened intently, her eyes wide with wonder. "But Daddy, what about you? Who will protect you while you're away?" she asked softly.

Hill smiled tenderly at his daughter. "You will, my darling," he said, brushing a strand of hair away from her face. "Your love and prayers will be my shield, no matter the distance between us. And always know that I carry you with me, in my heart, wherever I go."

Ci-Ci hugged her father tightly, feeling the weight of his words. "I love you, Daddy," she whispered.

"I love you too, Ci-Ci," Hill replied, his voice thick with emotion. "Now get some sleep, my brave little warrior. Tomorrow is a big day for both of us."

"You protect him and inspire him when the world is against him, and he decides to take a stance. God had a great creation in man, yet God's greatest creation of all time was you, the Woman," Hill said, his voice filled with pride and love as he hugged his daughter tightly and smiled at her while rubbing the left side of her face. "I love you, little woman," he told her.

"I love you too, goodnight, daddy," Ci-Ci replied softly.

Hill turned as he reached her door; he turned to see Ci-Ci get comfortable in her bed and whispered, "Until the next time, Ci-Ci."

Hill made his way back to the bed where Seaven had fallen asleep with tears running down her face. He walked around to ensure his home was secure before finally coming to bed. Seaven snored lightly as Hill got into bed. Pulling out his phone, he sent Helen a text. Hill fell asleep holding his wife's hand.

The alarm went off at 0430. Seaven hit the snooze but jumped up when she felt Hill get out of bed. "Hill, go ahead and shit, shower, and shave. I'll get breakfast ready," she said. Both Hill and Seaven checked on Ci-Ci before they went to their respective rooms for the morning routine. Seaven had Hill's favorite items laid out for him when he was ready for breakfast: bacon, cheese grits, Texas toast, cheese eggs, pork sausages, fruit, and orange juice. Hill was pleasantly surprised when he reached the dining room table. They ate and had a nice conversation before Hill had to put on his uniform.

"Are you sure you don't want us there today? Ci-Ci wants to see you off," Seaven asked.

"It's killing me to leave y'all like this. I can't handle having y'all there and having to command these Marines. You know I love y'all, right?" Hill responded.

"Yes, Hill, I do," Seaven signed, "You are my love."

Hill hugged and kissed his wife; she didn't want to let him go. "Baby, I must go to the garage to meet the Gunny."

When Gunny got to the garage, he spoke loudly: "Good morning, Sir, do you need help with anything else?"

"No, Gunny, everything else I need is already at the hangar," Hill responded.

After putting his gear in the bed of the truck, Hill hugged his wife, kissed her, and told her, "I love you, Seaven Rowe. I will be back in six months. Until then, take care of yourself and Ci-Ci." Seaven, with tears in her eyes, signed, "I love you," before she did an about-face and went back into their house.

...Ribs were chosen….......... ☐......(8)......

...you is who too…......... ☐......(9)......

Hill's deployment came and went with what seemed to be the blink of an eye; unfortunately, his six months turned into twelve months. During this time, he and Helen had drawn up divorce papers and forgotten about Rico. Seaven had been contacted by Rico, but she turned him down almost every time. Yet, she and Mai had become closer. On the last conversation she had with Rico, he told her, "Seaven, I may never see you again, so remember this from when we first kissed: Invigorating thoughts of you from time to time. Your captivating smile, your hypnotic eyes, and that body, that ass, aww so fine. While you may be losing your hearing, never be blind to those around you and how they occupy your time."

Seaven's voice cracked, and with tears in her eyes, she told him, "Rico, I had to go."

Tony had graduated high school, but he hadn't headed to college yet. Instead, Tony began his yearlong training to become a government-contracted assassin like Rico. While Tony was gone, his friends continued to come by the house to study and visit their second family. Leon and Tory loved this as they inadvertently learned lifelong lessons from each of Tony's friends.

Rich, the ladies' man, taught Leon how to dress for success and how to charm the ladies. Leon would see Rich in action when they went to the mall. Solo taught them when and how to be aggressive. Solo didn't speak much to people he didn't know, but when he did, others listened. They saw Solo get into a few fights, but they also saw him get out of just as many fights by speaking.

Rose taught them the power of words, lyrics, and how they could fight for them. She taught Tory how to use her beauty, combined with her wordplay, to get anything she wanted from men.

Rose taught them to think outside of the box and put together a list of songs they could use to their advantage. Leon and Rose would simply listen to and learn songs on some days. Leon had his first crush on Rose, the second most beautiful woman he knew.

Chris taught them to be humble even though they may have had more than others. He taught them to smile even when they didn't want to. They learned that sometimes their good deeds were better when no one else knew about them. They were both with Chris when he opened a 12ft trailer filled with food, fed the homeless for a few days, and put some of them to work on the truck, something no one knew about except Chris, Tory, and Leon.

Ken and Drea both taught them how to use their senses and those other senses they didn't know they had. Ken taught the little ones the importance of their vestibular sense or the sense of balance. He would play games they thought were impossible for anyone and encourage them to eat in the dark to not only enjoy food more but also notice the differences in spices. Drea would open their minds with the books she read to them and the science she showed them.

In secret, Drea told them one day she would not need the cane because she was going to invent robot hips and legs for people who used walking canes and wheelchairs, and before she died, she would be at least one step closer to curing herself. She taught the little ones to dream big and always have a plan. Leon saw Drea walk without her walking cane, and Tory ran with her. Tory and Leon would go to the mall with her as she tried on the latest fashion; some did not look good on her body, others Leon clearly loved and told her. She was the third most beautiful woman Leon had seen because she was so determined, so intelligent, and always wanted to learn more. They liked going to the mall with Ken because they guided Ken, but Ken made the choice of what to buy in the mall. When everyone could go to the mall together was the best day of the little ones' life.

When Tony returned from his African trip home, a duty all Cloven men took after high school, or that's what their friends believed. Tony, Ken, and a few of their friends headed to the same college. While some got a Bachelor's and others got a Master's degree, only one person would earn their PhD. Drea, or Dr. Dre as her friends called her, went on to get her Ph.D. in biotechnology and within a couple of years opened her own consulting firm. Drea would eventually be joined by Rose, Solo, Ken, and Chris to help form King Rose Consulting.

...you is who too….........▢......(9)......

……Take care........▢......(10)......

A few years later, Leon was at his cousin Man-Man's house, visiting when a block party started up.

Man-Man's sister Lisa rushed out of the house to meet up with an old friend who was visiting for the summer at the block party.

Man-Man and Leon talked and watched TV for about another hour before they headed out to the party.

Night had fallen so everyone was enjoying themselves even more because the music got a little louder.

Leon and Man-Man went to visit the guys cooking, then headed to the DJ booth.

Everyone commented on how Leon had grown and how he would be graduating high school at 16 years old.

In the blink of an eye, a fight broke out and a crowd gathered.

Man-Man called his sister Lisa to tell her and her friend to get back home.

Man-Man told Leon it was time for them to leave because you never knew who had a gun these days.

Man-Man gave another one of his friends daps as he and Leon headed for his home.

Then out of nowhere, they heard machine gun fire followed by the shots of a much less powerful gun.

Man-Man shouted, "Lisa, you better be at home."

Even though Man-Man was a few minutes younger than his twin sister, he acted like her father at times.

When the guys reached the house, they called for Lisa, but to their surprise, she didn't answer.

Leon said, "I'll go check the spot where we came from with the cars; you call the police and ambulance."

Leon sprinted back down from where they came, calling out for Lisa.

In mid-stride, Leon stopped in front of a Blue Chrysler 300. He looked to his left, but when he turned to his right, he could see Lisa and her friend. To his surprise, it was Sierra. They were signaling him to get down and come to them.

Before he could do so, footsteps approached. Leon instinctively got into a fighting stance as the young man approached him.

"A nigga who you rep," Leon said.

"A bru, I ain't from here. I don't rep nobody. I'm out cha looking for my fam, dawg," the young man responded.

"You betta get 'em 'cause we shooting somebody tonight, nigga," the young man warned.

"I got you, my nigga," Leon said as he turned his back.

The young man ran in the opposite direction, but before Leon could focus on Sierra, the thunderous boom from a gun was heard as Leon was thrown to the ground.

The first voice said, "What you doing, my nigga? He ain't one of them; dat nigga ain't even from here."

A second voice said, "I thought he was one of them; let's get outta here, my nigga, before 12 get here."

Leon was facing the girls as all this happened. Sierra went to help Leon, but he whispered, "No, not yet."

With his ear to the ground, he could hear the two young men running away.

"O.k., they're gone. Let's get y'all home," Leon said.

As he attempted to get up, he fell back down, but when his eyes opened, Sierra had his left hand and Lisa was gone.

"Sierra, are you O.K.?" Leon asked.

Sierra smiled, "Yes, why do you ask?"

"I can't think straight, Sierra, but before I lose woman Jubilation that slumbers humble as a mumble in this magnificent jungle. Sierra, you are mine…Mine to play…Mine to hold… Until the time after we are old… I am yours…Your shoulder to cry on…I am your warm body when you're cold."

As he lay there on his stomach, Sierra's cell phone played the drums of "Take Care" by Drake and Rihanna. Leon's eyes closed as he heard an ambulance approaching, the song echoing in the background, "If you let me, here's what I'll do…" He squeezed Sierra's hand as paramedics assessed him and attempted to communicate with him. Leon slipped in and out of consciousness but didn't let go of Sierra's hand as the song played each time his eyes opened.

Once in the ambulance, his eyes opened to the lyrics of the song, "They won't get you as I will, my only wish is I die real," his eyes closed. Leon could hear Sierra cry as his eyes opened, the music started again, and he heard the lyrics, "We'll change the pace and we'll just go slow, you won't ever have to worry, you won't ever have to hide." Leon squeezed Sierra's hand, their eyes met, he smiled just before his eyes closed.

As his eyes closed, he could hear the chorus of the song fading: "If you let me." Leon could hear the song more clearly as he opened his eyes: "Cause your mind doesn't control what it does sometimes, you hate being alone when you aren't the only one," were the lyrics now.

Leon could feel a vicious tug on his body as the song hit its second chorus: "Don't tell me, I don't care…" Thunderous drums played, and with his eyes partially open, he could see someone pulling Sierra away. This sent adrenaline rushing through his veins as he sat up and roared, "STOP!!!"

The entire room was quiet as Sierra pushed away from the male nurse who was holding her. Leon's eyes widened as he inhaled. His eyes locked on the male nurse as he exhaled and roared, and the room heard a low, deep roar that seemed to echo like a lion a mile away. Sierra rushed over to him, urging, "Look at me! Look at me, Leon! Lisa, help me! Release my hand!" She was confused, so she said the first thing that came to mind: "Release me, my lion!"

He tilted his head to his left as his eyes first examined Lisa, then they connected with Sierra on his right. "My lioness, are you okay? What are you bleeding, and where is that beeping sound, Lisa? Where is Man-Man?"

"Leon, I am okay, but look around, these doctors are here to help you; this is your blood," Sierra explained. "Man-Man is okay, Lee-Lee," Lisa explained, "but you have to listen to Sierra now. Call my father, Sierra, only you, no one else; use the blue card in my wallet," Leon said.

Sierra agreed but said, "Give me what is in your left hand." Leon's left hand hovered above her open hands as he released two different scalpels he had grabbed. "Leon, I'll be back when I call your father," Sierra handed the scalpels to the male nurse to her left. Lisa took his hand, while Sierra placed the palm of her hand on Leon's head and spoke, "Calm yourself, come little prince, and try to sleep now." Lisa and Sierra guided Leon's body onto the bed with the help of other nurses. Lisa and Sierra repeated the words: "We are okay, Lee-Lee, rest now, we are okay, Lee-Lee, rest now."

Leon lay down, but his eyes never left Sierra. Kissing her fingers and then placing them on his chest. A calming voice echoed as she looked him in his eyes and spoke: "Calm yourself, little prince… You are allowed to sleep now."

Leon looked at his cousin Lisa, "I can't, not yet…." Rico's voice could now be heard, "Son, you must rest now and listen to Lisa…." For a brief moment, only the beeping of the machine could be heard as Lisa spoke words that few in this room had heard. Lisa placed her hand on top of Sierra's hand that was resting on Leon's chest, her feminine voice spoke: Our Fadduh awt'n Hebb'n, all-duh-weh be dy holy 'n uh rightschus name. Dy kingdom com.' Oh lawd leh yo' holy 'n rightschus woud be done, on dis ert' as-'e tis dun een yo'grayt Hebb'n. 'N ghee we oh Lawd dis day our day-ly bread. \"N f'gib we oh Lawd our trus-passes, as we alsp f'gib doohs who com' sin 'n trupass uhgehs us. \"N need-us-snot on konkuhrin' King een tub no moh ting like un sin 'n eeb'l, Fuh dyne oh dyne is duh kingdom 'n duh kingdom prommus fuh be we-ebbuh las' n glory. Amen

As the prayer ended, Leon's breathing calmed, his eyes slowly closed, and finally, he drifted off again.

After learning of his son's injuries, Rico sent a doctor he trusted to help operate. Tony did the same an hour later. Within 12 hours of arriving at the hospital, Leon had one of the lead brain surgeons and one of the leading cosmetic surgeons at his bedside. Within seven days of arriving at the hospital, Leon was cleared to leave. Luckily, his brain was not hit by the bullet. While Leon would go through three more surgeries over the next year, during these next two weeks Sierra barely left his side.

Man-Man and Lisa teased their puppy love but enjoyed seeing Leon happy. People came to visit Man-Man, Lisa, Sierra, and Leon during his stay. Lisa pulled Sierra aside one day to tell her about Leon's mother, who she truly was, how she died, and what Leon had faced growing up. Man-Man told Leon that Sierra's mother was single for a while and once she found out what happened, she would more than likely come to get Sierra because she worried so much.

On the Wednesday before she was to leave, Leon professed his love for Sierra. They began to touch; their bodies got hot but before they could make love, Lisa ran into the basement to tell Sierra her mother had arrived early. She told Leon, "Go outside because Sierra's mom thinks she is down here looking at TV with me." Leon reluctantly did as he was told.

In the morning, as the sun began to rise, Leon prepared for his day and went to sit on the front porch, waiting for his cousins and the sun to wake up. Leon had a feeling he needed to get off the porch and walk towards Sierra's cousin's home. When he was about three houses away, Sierra burst out of the door, running to and hugging him. Through her tears, she told him she was leaving. Sierra held him tight and whispered, "I love you, my Lion. I touched myself last night with thoughts of you."

Seaven came outside to see her daughter hugging a young man. Before rushing to her child, she asked her sister who the young man was. Seaven was told that Leon was the boy who took a bullet for Sierra and Lisa. Seaven's eyes widened as she hesitated and asked what his name was and who his family was. Seaven's sister said they called him Lion because they said he roared at the nurse for touching Sierra and almost killed a man who was holding Lisa back. "Your daughter and Lisa were the only ones to calm him before his brain surgery. Lisa spoke in a different language that calmed the Lion," she explained.

Seaven said, "This can't be." Her sister touched her shoulder, stood in front of her, and signed, "I could not hear you. Say again." Seaven smiled and said, "Don't worry," and added, "Lisa was speaking a golden language called Gullah." The sister asked how

Seaven could possibly know this. Seaven signed, "The Lion was taught Gullah as a child, but if he is here, I can't be," then she walked outside.

Seaven approached the young couple, saying, "Leon, Prince Leon."

Sierra couldn't believe what she was hearing, so she turned and began to sign to her mother. Seaven signed back.

Leon said, "Ma'am, I enjoy your speech."

Seaven rushed to and hugged Leon tightly. "I remember you, ma'am. Are you okay? Where is your little girl? I don't remember her name," Leon inquired.

Seaven spoke in her unbalanced voice, "Thank you, young Prince, for saving my daughter again, but we must leave you once more."

Sierra pushed past her mother to kiss her Lion. "I'm ready to go now, Mom," Sierra said, before her mother's boyfriend approached them.

Sierra's mother's male friend began to escort the ladies back to their SUV when a thought came to Leon that caused him to whisper it over and over. Then he shouted, "MA'AM!!!"

Sierra stopped as she made her mother turn when Leon

looked up to the sky, whispering something. His eyes connected with Seaven's eyes when he said, "Invigorating thoughts…"

She read his lips, then she ran to him, pulling Sierra with her. When they approached Leon, Seaven tapped her lips with her fingers.

Sierra said, "Repeat that, Leon."

His eyes fixated on Seaven as he repeated, "Invigorating thoughts of you from time to time…" His attention shifted to Sierra as he continued, "Sierra, your magical smile, amazing eyes, and infectious personality. One day, you will be with me."

Their paths wouldn't pass again for two years, until Sierra reached the age of 19.

……Take Care……. □……(10)……
……Echo……. □……(11)……

On the day before her 19th birthday, Sierra took a flight back to Georgia to visit her blond-haired, blue-eyed boyfriend Michael and her best friend Alexis.

Alexis picked her up at the airport and gave her an early birthday gift: a white gold necklace with a pendant that was Sierra's birthstone, shaped like a heart. The hour drive back to Alexis's apartment was filled with stories of people who had entered Alexis's life and those she had brushed off.

Once in Alexis's apartment, Sierra just wanted to rest because her week was filled with tests. When she woke an hour later, Alexis had prepared some appetizers and picked out a nice dinner dress for Sierra to wear. Alexis told Sierra she wanted to take her out on a date and that the guys would join them later.

Sierra first met some of Alexis's new friends at a bar that was full of females. Sierra noticed this and asked Alexis why this was. Alexis explained: "Well, I didn't know how to tell you this, but I like women too. I just didn't want to lose you as a friend if you found out from someone else."

Sierra smiled and said, "Alexis, you are my friend and I accept you for who you are, all of you. I love you, girl." Alexis hugged her with a tear coming from her eyes, telling Sierra she was only the third person to accept her; everyone else disapproved or left her. Sierra confessed to exploring women too.

The ladies had a few drinks as Sierra was hit on by a few of the ladies. Alexis told them she was off-limits, and they all pretended to cry. Sierra enjoyed the fact that her friend came out to her.

Alexis and Sierra were followed to the party on campus by a little convoy of vehicles. Once they reached the party, Alexis found her boyfriend Sam within five minutes. He, in turn, called Michael to inform him the ladies had arrived.

While waiting for Michael at the bar, Sierra got a strange feeling of calm and comfort. She thought it was the drinks, so she hugged Michael when he approached. He introduced her to a few of his friends as they walked and talked.

Sierra noticed one female following them and paying attention to every move they made. She stopped and asked Michael about the blonde-haired, green-eyed girl. He said she was just a friend as he pulled Sierra through the doors of the building where people had begun dancing. Sierra stopped him as her heart began to beat faster, causing her to breathe faster and lose her balance. She told Michael, "Give me a minute; I think I'm having an anxiety attack." Michael left her outside and proceeded to the party.

As she took a seat outside, her nose tasted the air as a group of men walked past her. As they sat down, she thought she saw Leon. Sierra rubbed her eyes to make sure it was him. When she realized it was him, her mouth opened, for the man she saw before her was the boy she had dreamed of.

In the midst of his conversation, Leon stopped and stood up. His nose tested the air as he turned toward Sierra with his eyes closed. When his eyes opened, they were attached to Sierra's dark almond brown skin and her wide eyes. Without hesitation, the two met, they hugged as Leon kissed her neck whispering: "Happy birthday, beautiful."

"I can't," Sierra whispered, "I have a boyfriend, Leon. How long have you had that problem?" Leon asked. Sierra smiled, saying, "No, he is o.k.. He is good to me." Leon said, "Cool, can I meet him? I want to see this man."

"Leon, I thought you went to the Marines," Sierra asked.

"I did. I'm on leave visiting one of my friends who got out, so which one is your man?"

Sierra was simply amazed at how Leon had changed, even the way he smelled was turning her on. "Leon," she said, "why are you trying to fight when we just came back together? I want you," she corrected herself, "I mean, I need you to chill out."

"Girl, I don't want to fight him, I just want to meet my competition, oh and I want you too. Let's go back to my hotel room."

His attention was squarely on her when he said: "Sierra, your magical smile, amazing eyes, and infectious personality, one day, you will be with me."

For just a moment, Sierra could feel herself being pulled closer to Leon. She could smell his breath and damn near hear his heartbeat. Her magnetism pulled Leon closer as he smelled her hair, he did everything in his power to stop moving closer to this woman.

At that moment, Michael rushed outside shouting: "WHO THE FUCK is this, Sierra? Who is this guy?"

So caught up in each other, they didn't even hear Michael until he repeated himself.

"Leon says I don't want any trouble, man; I was just speaking to an old friend, no disrespect."

Michael smiled and said, "No, you can have her black ass, because I knew she wanted a black guy. Fuck her, look what I got me," as he pointed to the female from earlier. He kissed her passionately and slapped her ass.

"See, Sierra, I have friends too, and guess what? Cindy puts out a lot more than you. See, this happens when you want to study more than fuck me."

Sierra turned around, sobbing softly as the crowd that had gathered got quiet. Leon pulled Sierra close, and with his eyes squarely on Michael, he whispered, "My Lioness, protect yourself ……….. or I will."

With this, Sierra wiped her face and straightened her dress before turning around. Alexis and her crew had arrived at this time. Sierra spoke, "I am a lady, and before I lose my cool, I will take a step back and allow you to do as you please."

Alexis shouted, "No, Sierra, get him and that white bitch!" Sierra smiled. There was a pause, and then she spoke again, "Any man at this party, straight or gay, I can take home with me tonight, and they will gladly take a bullet or fight for me. All I need to do is ask."

"Alexis, there was only one man there who had taken a bullet for me and saved my life without a second thought. That man's very presence sent chills down my spine. When he spoke, my knees got weak, and his touch got my pussy wet. My pu nan e pulsated when he recited my name..."

The crowd said "DAMMM" in unison as Sierra continued.

"Michael, my dear," she said with a smile as she got closer to him. She stroked the tiny hairs on Cindy's arm and exhaled as the two women came face to face. Sierra continued, "Michael, your Cindy had fallen into his spell already, but you were too foolish to realize it. Look at her lips, wet and trembling. Look at her pulling her hair back. Now watch her hands as she squeezed her stomach."

The crowd's awe and appreciation grew as they watched Cindy do everything Sierra described. Her legs couldn't even stop moving, her breaths were getting deeper, her tits rose and fell quicker as her nipples hardened.

"And to think he hadn't even touched her yet. Michael, you wanted to see what that man was capable of, you ignoramus," Sierra said as she caught Cindy's attention. Her eyes instructed her to hold Leon and watch how his warm hands went down her back and grabbed her ass.

The crowd's reactions varied as everything Sierra described happened in the most sultry ways. Most couldn't believe their eyes, and others touched themselves.

"Watch her head fall into his other hand, his cheek will touch hers as he whispers sweet nothings in her ear. Now look… the only words that could be heard were Cindy moaning... Look at her body attempting to attach itself to him, her eyes closed. Now, watch her underwear come from under her dress. Now watch your little bitch of a man, how on my command she lost it."

Leon had this woman in his grasp, squeezing her tits, stroking her clit, and kissing her neck and ears. Sierra's bedroom eyes looked at Michael as she walked behind Cindy, stroking the inside of her thigh as her body moved with Leon's steady strokes. She then walked behind Leon as Cindy and Leon's bodies interfered with her view of Michael for just a second.

Sierra reached Leon's left shoulder, kissing his neck ever so gently, and whispered loud enough for others to hear, "Attack…"

Leon squeezed the woman's tits, then her stomach, and then squeezed her ass. In a circular motion, he rubbed the inside of her thighs, then he pressed his warm hands under her dress and stroked her clit. Within 15 seconds, she became stiff as a board. Leon forcefully turned Cindy so that Michael could see the beads of sweat cover her body as liquid from her body rushed down her leg and onto the ground. Her stomach tightened when Leon whispered into her ear, "Cindy, you sexy bitch, it's time to go," he whispered, a tear fell from her eye when Leon released her to her friends.

Pushing her friends away, Cindy threw her petite body against Leon, whispering, "Oh my god, please, no." Sierra licked her lower lip, saying, "Yes…" The crowd instantly got quiet, no one dared to move. "Cindy, don't say a fucking word until I say so," Leon whispered. Cindy moved her head up and down as his warm breath then his lips caressed her forehead, his lips next briefly met her lips, now his lips stroked her cheek as he whispered, "You don't speak, woman," simultaneously his warm, manly hands descended on her body, the warmth of his hands penetrating the dress she wore.

Leon's lips now reached her neck. Then as his hands reached her ass, his lips kissed her cleavage, his warm breath keeping her nipples at attention. He counted, "1 Mississippi, 2 Mississippi, 3 Mississippi," by the fourth second, she couldn't hold out any more and yelled out in pleasure. "Shut YOUR ass up!!!" Leon demanded.

Cindy's body went limp as his finger stroked her clit harder. Leon whispered something in her ear that brought life back to her body. Her hips were in sync with his warm hand. She stuttered saying, "Okay, okay."

Three seconds passed when her eyebrows went to the top of her head, she shook her head side to side and requested to be put down. When her feet touched the ground, she grabbed Leon's hand, placing it around her throat and making him squeeze. When his two wet fingers exited her lower region, they went immediately to stroking just below her belly button. She looked at him sincerely, and smiled as her eyes rolled back, she forcefully squirted on her dress before she could pull it up and finish on the grass.

Leon said to her, "Speak, Cindy…"

Her friends had to help her back to her dorm room because she stumbled like a drunken person trying to walk, her legs still jerking, her stomach still tightening, and her body covered in sweat.

"Michael, my dear, you can have her because that man, who risked his life without a second thought, just did to her in 45 seconds what you couldn't do to me in our entire relationship," Sierra said, squirting hand sanitizer in Leon's hands before she grabbed him and pulled him closer, their eyes connecting as the crowd was still eerily quiet.

Leon kissed her forehead, allowing her to smell him, and then his right cheek rubbed her cheek. Sierra whispered, "Not tonight, Leon."

Leon smiled at Michael as he whispered, "Tomorrow then," before he and Sierra's lips passionately connected for a moment, then separated, turning their backs to the crowd and walking off.

The crowd went wild with disbelief, amazement, and joy. Michael and his crew ran toward the couple but were stopped by the 5 Marines Leon was with. Sierra stopped, turned around, then pointed and laughed at Michael, saying you honestly thought you could hurt me.

"You bitch, you black bitch, I will get you," Michael shouted as his crew took him away. Alexis and Sam approached Sierra as Leon stopped.

Sam said, "I didn't know, honest,"

Alexis insisted, "Let's go get him."

"Are you okay with leaving Sierra?" Leon asked.

Sierra smiled, her eyes sparkling as she shook her head up and down, "Wait… where are you going, Leon?"

"I have to get my brothers and sisters before someone gets hurt, we will be better off at the hotel," Leon said.

Sierra's head bowed slightly as she coughed, swiftly Leon began to walk past her, yet his essence engulfed Sierra for a moment.

His scent filled her nostrils, his warm breath on the back of her neck saying, "Come here, magnificent you," causing her fist to ball up, her shoulder to roll back causing, her perky breast to rise, her ass to rise, her body to lift itself onto her tiptoes, she couldn't breathe, yet she didn't struggle.

Those in close proximity's eyes widened as they witnessed a woman damn near possessed with desire, spin 180 degrees and all at once... She exhaled, her body relaxed, eyes closed, inhaling through her nose, eyes opened, exhaling through her mouth. Gently Leon's tongue fucked her mouth, her hands didn't know where to touch him, in between breaths, he whispered, "Magnificent you, I have to go, I have to go."

Pulling away, he smiled, saying, "For now, go." Walking back to the crowd, Leon looked to compose himself. Then as his eyes rose up, all commotion stopped; no one dared to move as all eyes focused on Leon as he stepped closer. Alexis's question, "Sierra, look, they all stopped."

Sam, confused, asked, "Dam, what did he do?"

Sierra was fixated on the way Leon commanded everyone's attention without uttering a single word, Sierra loved the way his ass looked in his jeans, and his shoulders had her biting her lower lip. Alexis began to speak again but did a double-take when she noticed how Sierra's eyes were stalking Leon.

With his hands cupped around his mouth in a commanding, deep bass-filled voice, Leon shouted out, "DEVIL DOGS...." his words echoed for a few seconds before every Marine at the party, old, young, man, and woman, those who came with him and those in attendance answered with a thunderous OHHRAH, heard throughout the campus....Leon's response, "EYEBALLS," in unison, the 5 Marines Leon came with and the 40 others at the party responded with an even louder and more thunderous and sharp SNAP!!! All Marines' eyes were focused squarely on Leon. Everyone in the crowd was amazed at what they were seeing because some had never seen this, while others were excited to see what came next.

Leon slapped his chest twice, shouting, "ECHO," the younger Marines looked confused, but an older Marine who happened to be in the middle of the crowd responded loudly, "ECHO SIR." Leon shouted, "ON THE COMMAND TO FALLOUT," the Echo Marine said, "ON FALLOUT...." Leon, "MEET ME AT BALLROOM KILO UNDERGROUND," Echo Marine, "BALLROOM KILO UNDERGROUND...." Leon, "AT HOTEL FAIRMONT ONE," Echo Marine, "FAIRMONT 1...." Leon began,

"FALLL!!!," Echo Marine joined him saying, "FALLL!!!," They both ended with a sharp, "OUT!!!!"

"Y'all might want to move," Leon said as he smiled at Sierra and her crew. Within seconds, about 150 people ran past them shouting, grunting, and pointing in the direction of the hotel. Some ran the 2 miles to the hotel, while others convoyed there. The Echo Marine approached Leon to shake his hand. "You know, Marine, I think I'm the only one who knows that cadence here," he said as he shook Leon's hand. He asked, "So how do you plan on pulling that off, that many people at that fancy hotel?"

Leon said, "Sir, I know the owner's family, plus they were ready for us." Echo Marine said, "Us? You all didn't want an old-timer like me there, did ya?" Leon smiled and said, "Once a Marine, always a Marine." "Sir, bring some of your buddies down tonight. My sisters, brothers, and I left in a week for our first deployment, so come see us off." Echo Marine's cheeks turned red as he smiled. "We will be there in about an hour, and who do we report to?"

"Lance Corporal Leon Cloven, sir."

"Aye, Lance Corporal."

Sierra waited for Leon to finish talking before she approached him, asking for a ride to the hotel. "What about your friends? Are they coming?" "They left me here to find my own ride, those fuckers," Sierra said, smiling. "Do you really know the owner, my Lion?"

"Yes, my lioness, just listen," Leon called his childhood friend Chris to inform him of how many people were on their way and to expect a group of older Marines to show up in an hour or so.

"Thank you, Leon. You all enjoy the space. I've got everything you asked for. Oh, do you still need your suite?"

"Yes, please, Chris."

"Got it, Lee-Lee. I'll see you in a bit, little dude."

On the ride over, Leon explained to Sierra that he would be leaving in a week, but he didn't want her to wait on him. He wanted her to enjoy her life and just think of him as the man who would always be there for her.

Sierra and Leon entered the party unnoticed and had a few minutes alone to catch up on the past couple of years before the 5 Marines who came with Leon sat in a semi-circle around his table to stop people from disturbing their conversation. Each Marine had a date and took turns dancing and acting a fool while the other Marines and their dates stayed in the semi-circle.

For about an hour, Sierra and Leon were not disturbed as they continued to smile, flirt, and catch up on the good times. Chris came downstairs with Echo Marine and his crew approaching Leon.

"Lee-Lee, this is SSgt Elms (a.k.a. Echo Marine) and his Marines." SSgt Elm's crew was as diverse as America. Their ages ranged from 21 to 75. They were gay and straight, young and old, fat and skinny, and were all races. This crew had a case of vodka in tow. They were integrated into the party, and because SSgt Elms still had his motorcycle helmet in hand, LCpl Lisa Perez (from Leon's crew) asked if she could attach a GoPro camera to it and if she could wear it for a little while. SSgt Elm's wife agreed to allow the young Marine to wear the helmet for a little while.

The helmet was passed from person to person for the rest of the night. SSgt Elmes and his wife sat with Sierra, Leon, and Chris for a little while, talking about life in the military. Chris told stories about Leon when he was a kid, about his little brother Lee-Lee, and how he always hung out with his brother Tony and the older crew. He told about how beautiful Leon's mother was and how Lee-Lee's dad helped open the hotel they were in now.

As the party came to an end, a line of cabs and rideshare vehicles awaited the drunken students, staff, and Marine vets. Chris approached SSgt Elms and his wife to tell them the hotel had a few rooms available if he and his buddies and their wives wanted to stay. SSgt Elms hesitated at first, so Chris smiled and told him they were all at the house. Mrs. SSgt Elms said, "Yes, we will take a room, and our pals need rooms too."

Leon pulled Sierra to the side and told her, "I don't want to see you tomorrow because I want to remember your smile as is now. I don't want my last image of you to be a sad occasion."

He handed her the keys to the Cadillac Escalade that they drove to the hotel in. They hugged for a moment, a moment longer, before Sierra smiled and told Leon to come home safe. Leon went to his suite and prepared for bed.

Sierra drove back to Alexi's apartment, happy to have seen Leon, excited that he had saved her again, and saddened to know he would be at war in only a few days.

Sierra tried to sleep, but her hormones did not allow her to stop thinking about Leon. Her night is interrupted more when she heard Alexi in the next room having sex with her boyfriend and her new girlfriend.

Sierra began to sweat; the louder the moans got, her panties got wet as she heard Sam protesting. After a few minutes, she couldn't take it anymore. She put on her yoga pants and nightshirt, bursting into the room to catch a glimpse of the threesome that she was hearing, it only provoked her more. Alexis and her new girlfriend enticed Sierra to join, but she couldn't . Her body only wanted one person, and now she knew where he was, and how to get to him, and she had the transportation to do so.

"Alexis, I have to, I have to go… I will see you in the morning. Please call me if you get worried. Oh my god, Alexis, I have to find this man."

……Echo........ □......(11)......

…Steamy shower…......... □......(12)......

Standing in line at the busy hotel, Sierra could overhear a conversation about a game where someone was caught on camera doing a prank. She entered the conversation by telling the group she had a few friends on websites that did that type of work and could help them get more viewership if they needed it. They got out of line to speak with Sierra about the possibility of renting some equipment for a task they were assigned to perform. They wanted to become Vaultmen but wanted to rent some video equipment vice buying it.

"What is a Vaultman?" she asked, but only got vague answers.

She got some of their contacts and wished them good hunting for the night. Reaching the front desk of the hotel, Sierra was greeted by the clerk: "Ma'am, here is the key to your suite. I was told you would be back. Enjoy your night."

Slightly confused, Sierra took the elevator to the 30th floor.

Jumping off the elevator, she rushed into Leon's suite. Opening the door, she could see steam coming from the bathroom. Leon, donning only a towel, signaled her over to the shower. With his remote, he turned on a mixtape Rose made him.

As Rose's mixtape played in the background, "What took your sexy ass so long?" he whispered.

"Fuck you, sir," she said with a smile.

"I need to shower you first," he whispered again, "No, not my hair baby, you know you can't touch a black woman's hair."

"Fuck your hair, Sierra, get out of those clothes, and get that sexy ass in my steamy shower." Sierra did as she was told. Leon removed his towel, placing it on the floor just outside of the shower. He started at her toes, then washed every inch of her magnificently thick body. He purposely wet her hair when he came to her feet, placing her back against his stomach and chest. Her wet hair fell just below her breast. Leon bent down to rub her soaked breast, pressing his chest against her back, kissing her neck as his dick rose in between her ample ass cheeks. Leon's pulsating dick teased Sierra when he began to rinse all the soap from her body.

"Put your hands here and arch your back," Sierra did as she was told.

Leon entered her warm abyss, causing her to moan and clench up.

"Fuck you, sir," she said with a smile.

"I need to shower you first," he whispered again, "No, not my hair baby, you know you can't touch a black woman's hair."

"Fuck your hair, Sierra, get out of those clothes, and get that sexy ass in my steamy shower." Sierra did as she was told. Leon removed his towel, placing it on the floor just outside of the shower. He started at her toes, then washed every inch of her magnificently thick body. He purposely wet her hair when he came to her feet, placing her back against his stomach and chest. Her wet hair fell just below her breast. Leon bent down to rub her soaked breast, pressing his chest against her back, kissing her neck as his dick rose in between her ample ass cheeks. Leon's pulsating dick teased Sierra when he began to rinse all the soap from her body.

"Take this dick, you sexy bitch," Leon said as he entered her, causing her to moan and clench up. Sierra could only make grown woman sounds as Leon gave her an inch at a time. Pulling her wet hair as the water stopped, Sierra grabbed Leon's dick as he continued to thrust into her deeper. For just a moment, her thirst was quenched. Leon grabbed both her wrists, pulling them behind her as he got a little deeper. Sierra's moans echoed in the bathroom. Leon pulled out, and for a moment, Sierra continued to moan. He brought her body close; "Let's get out now, my beautiful lioness." Sierra did as she was told.

Starting at the top of her hips, traveling to her neck, while his lips traveled to her belly button, nibbling on the caramel brown skin just below her navel, his right hand squeezed her inner thighs. His left hand, just two fingers, entered her mouth; she grabbed his hands, sucking on his two fingers, sloppy sucking his fingers as his lips finally reached her clit. Removing his lubricated fingers from her mouth as saliva dropped off his finger, they hovered down her body, and slowly, each finger entered her. Her pussy massaged his fingers as her clit and his lips kissed passionately.

His right hand attacked her breasts as her loud exhales turned to seductive moans of pleasure mixed with a hint of pain. Her hips began to whine, her stomach muscles tightened as she first pulled her hair back, rubbed her face, her hands grabbed his right hand guiding it from breast to breast. Licking her lips, she released his hand as her focus was on his eyes. Her eyes went from looking pleased to angry. Grabbing his head, she forcefully ground his face into her body when she spoke quietly, whispering, "Eat dat pussy."

Her body began to glisten, and beads of sweat covered her sexy thick body. Leon stopped suddenly with a glazed face. He looked up and smiled; "Hell no, get yo ass back down der," Sierra shouted, grabbing his head and thrusting her wet pussy into his face. Leon surprised her as his fingers worked her pussy and his tongue worked her clit. She shouted obscenities until he rolled, then vibrated his tongue on her clit, squeezed her breast, and pulled his fingers toward his chin. Sierra's eyes closed as her body stiffened like a board, and for a moment, her soul left her body.

All were quiet when Sierra opened her eyes. She felt herself floating towards the ceiling. As she got close, she turned to see her body arch up, her arms outstretched, and her fingers giving praise. She heard someone harmonizing "Amen, Amen, Amen" as the chorus of the song "Take Me to Church" by Hozier continued. Her soul raced back to her body, "Take me to church. I'll worship like a dog at the shrine of your lies. I'll tell you my sins, and you can sharpen your knife, Offer me that deathless death, Good God, let me give you my life."

Sierra's eyes widened, and she exhaled, her body relaxed as her ears were filled with the melodies of Prince's "Call My Name." When her soul returned, she screamed in pleasure as Leon continued to eat her out, wrapping her legs around him and squeezing while seconds passed, then unknowingly, her body gave way to a flood of pleasure. Losing her composure for a moment, her toes pointed just before her knees bent.

"I have committed a sin," she thought as tears began to roll down her face. Her body glistened when her legs viciously shook involuntarily for just a moment. As his tongue pressed against her clit and his fingers went deep while tapping and pulling towards his chin, Leon's fingers slid out of her pussy as his tongue simultaneously began touching those hairs on her stomach, then rushing to her breast.

Sierra pulled him close, saying, "Why, why did you do me like this?"

On that bed, their dance continued for just an hour or so more. "Mi Amor" was recited by both Sierra and Leon.

She could feel his lips move up to her chin and then her lips, parting them with his tongue, with slow, deep kisses, growing more intense. Leon now got to experience the evolution of Sierra's face. For just a moment, his eyes traced the curvature of her thick figure, in which his tongue would taste. Sierra smiled while opening those majestically Egyptian eyes as the song "Requiem for a Dream" could be heard. Leon's baritone voice slipped from his chest, onto her breast, before her ears were laid to rest hearing him call out to her, "come"… "Come"… resisting him with an almost silent "no".

Forcefully, he placed both her wrists on the purple pillow, strategically placed to the left behind her head. The tiny hairs on Leon's right cheek tickled Sierra's right cheek when he whispered, "I want you… give to me what you dare not give another"... For a brief moment, the music could be heard before their cheeks rubbed together. Leon could feel Sierra smile then she spoke in a voice that entangled his intangible soul, causing his chin to rise as though he were a wolf howling to his lover, the moon. His shoulders attempted to touch one another just before releasing as his pectoral muscles flexed and were covered in goosebumps. Sierra's sexy voice spoke, saying simply, "Stop it," just before she sank her teeth into his flexed chest, awakening him to enter this contest.

Leon moaned, a slight roar escaping his lips. His attention fell on the sweet smell of her natural hair, "Do I dare?"

Releasing her wrist just before he glided his fingers through her drying hair. Gently pulling her hair, their eyes connected again just before his lips attacked her neck. His warm tongue caressed her neck before cool air was blown. Sierra's magnificent breast mounds of pleasure were awakened when lips sucked her right nipple as a warm hand squeezed and pulled the nipple on the left….

The music changed to the song "Call My Name" performed by Morgan James… And at the same time, his lips caressed her lips as his hands continued to enjoy those healthy breasts…. Sierra's head glided side to side before lips jumped from her lips onto her stomach, and teeth pulled at her tiny hairs. Sierra's magnificent body was Leon's fiesta, his fest, and a new song began. Mikki Howard's "Love Under New Management" began the moment Leon's lips reached a malnourished vessel.

Removing his lips, Leon's manhood entered, and she gasped for air, squeezing Leon's wrist, guiding one hand to squeeze her breast and the other to squeeze her neck.

"Give to me what you dare not give another, give me all of you," he whispered, as Leon gave her inches 2, 3, 4...

"Umm, more," were the words that escaped Sierra's lips in between moans of pleasure. Giving her inches 5 and 6 got her mouth to open and her eyes to close, shaking her head side to side still whispering, "noo noo no."

Thrusting into her an inch or two more, giving her all he had to offer, for just a moment, then pulling out, she screamed out; "not now."

Replacing his thick, long, and throbbing dick with his long, talent-warm tongue, Sierra began to sing out from the depth of her lungs....

Squeezing her ass cheeks as he lost himself in her pot of gold, just a moment more before her body shake, rattled, and rolled...

And just as quickly as she orgasmed on Leon's tongue, there was a new song, Luther Vandross' "If Only for One Night," played in the background as he grabbed Sierra's hips, forcing her to spin, pressing her stomach to the bed, massaging her legs, sliding ever so cautiously in between those sexy thighs.

Leon began hitting that ass from the back. Sierra could hear the remix of "Oh, I think they like me," when Leon came to his feet, getting deeper into her warm abyss, Sierra hollered out even though she tried to resist. Sierra spread her ass cheeks for Leon to get a bit deeper. Leon hollered out as he felt himself about to explode; he grabbed Sierra's wrist as he thrust harder, deeper, and faster into her pulsated-shaven pussy. Their moans of pleasure sounded like pain when Leon screamed out Sierra's full name.

At that moment Sierra rose, her shoulder coming up, as her back fell against Leon's chest. She grabbed his ass as he thrust deeper into her, wrapping his arms around her as he finally came, but Sierra wouldn't let him pull out. Pushing her ample ass against him as his dick attempted to go down. Leon screamed out, "Sierra, noo, girl, woman, what are you doing?" When she released him, he fell to the bed with his dick facing the ceiling.

Sierra's warm tongue attacked every inch of his manhood. She began sucking his dick, which had since been resurrected. Leon attempted to push her away, but she fought him off in his weakened state. "Give me this dick, Leon," Sierra cried, her eyes looking up to this man who refused to be taken advantage of. Grabbing his dick with both hands, sucking him off, all while looking into his soul, got her the reaction she was looking for; Leon almost cried as he attempted to sit up.

"Lay your fine ass down, Sierra," commanded Leon, "no Sierra you can't do me like this." Sierra straddled him, putting them in a 69 position. Leon could only lay back and enjoy the scene laid before him as her sexy ass rose and fell as she continued to suck his dick. Leon attempted to lick Sierra's pussy but decided to bite her ass cheeks and toss her salad. When Leon's tongue rubbed against Sierra's asshole, his dick was put to the back of Sierra's throat.

Leon motorboated Sierra's ass as she continued deep-throating his dick. Leon's toes curled when he felt another nut coming on. He attempted to fight back, but Sierra placed her calves under his shoulders and forced her ass into his face as he began to nut. A loud cry of pleasure escaped Leon as he was powerless against the sorcery this woman possessed.

"Sierra, you know you're wrong," Sierra smiled, "um, you taste good, what's the next song?" Together, they fell asleep, both snoring, tired and weak from the performance they had just put on.

Sierra was saddened to awaken in bed by herself, but Leon had left a video asking her to move on and enjoy life, and explaining the SUV was hers and that she would need to take it to a specific address to have it transferred to her name.

When Sierra checked out at the front desk, she saw the people from the night before at the hotel's restaurant. Some looked disheveled, and they all looked spooked, and she noticed two people looked to have something red on their clothes. She approached to ask if they had decided to pull the prank and to inform the young lady she had spilled something red on herself. They only spoke for a quick moment, and she learned the young lady with the red stain was preparing to be a Vaultman, but the group gave vague answers as to what a Vaultman was. Sierra left but stopped at a gas station to pick up a quick snack, just as the sun was coming over the horizon.

Getting out of her SUV, Sierra admired the sunrise when she saw what appeared to be a bloody body. She called the police to report what she was seeing and remembered the group speaking about a man who fit the dead man's description. Once the police arrived, Sierra explained to them how she came to see the body and what she had heard from the people at the hotel. More police and ambulances arrived as police were instructed to go find the group at the hotel.

Within 30 minutes, one of the people from the group was brought back to the scene of the murder. He began to confess what he knew to the police. Sierra could hear bits and pieces of what he was confessing, but she was saddened to see a life taken. They gave the older gentleman a cigarette and a few minutes to walk around because he could barely believe he witnessed everything that happened a few hours earlier.

Out of nowhere, loud gunshots could be heard as the older

gentleman was hit with a hail of bullets. The vehicle sped away as the older gentleman took his last breath in front of the crowd that had gathered. After this happened, Sierra was allowed to leave as the police started an investigation.

Leon entered a firefight a month after stepping foot into the country. A convoy of vehicles from his command was misdirected and taken hostage. Rico, Tony, and Leon were authorized to retrieve these vehicles and Marines because amongst the hostages was one of their fellow assassins.

……Steamy shower........ □......(12)......

……Jasper Jones........ □......(13)......

After parking her vehicle and walking to a Civic Center for an event, Tory read a homeless man's sign that read: "I, Jasper Jones, am asking you for any change you can spare. Thank you, and may God bless you and yours." She dropped him a few dollars as she continued to her destination.

Jasper walked a few blocks to his Mercedes GLE, which was parked behind a building. He did this in a few other areas around the city until night fell. As he began walking to his vehicle for the last time that day, he was approached by a young man who handed him a one-hundred-dollar bill. As Jasper turned to thank the young man, he blacked out.

Jasper was awakened by what sounded like glass breaking on a cement floor. To his right was a table with a note and bullets. His feet and hands were bound, and he was gagged; he struggled and screamed for help. "SHUT UP YOU BUM!!!!" was shouted back at him, then the voice began a monologue: "My name is Kramer Craigs, I gave the bum $100, then I knocked him out, I've brought him to an abandoned warehouse, I'm going to shoot him in the head then leave a suicide note. This is my application for the Vaultmen. My address is 555 Wesley Ave."

Kramer set his portable studio kit in front of Jasper. Releasing Jasper's left hand, Kramer accidentally released his right hand as well. A fight ensued, and Jasper got the upper hand and knocked Kramer on his ass. In doing this, Jasper was forced to the ground because his bound feet were coming free. Kramer, dazed and in a panic, reached for his gun and shot in Jasper's direction. The sight of Jasper's blood caused Kramer to vomit. His eyes widened and his mouth became ajar at what he was witnessing as he looked in Jasper's direction.

……Jasper Jones…… □ *……(13)……*

About The Author

Darrick Calvin, aged 45, is a devoted father of three and a proud military veteran. With 13 years of active duty in the Marine Corps and 8 years of Reserve service in the Army Reserves, Darrick's dedication to serving his country is undeniable. Having retired from the military, he has embarked on a new journey, currently pursuing his bachelor's degree in human resources.

Writing has been a lifelong passion for Darrick, serving as both a creative outlet and a tool for personal growth. He discovered his talent for poetry at the young age of six, using it as a means to overcome his stutter. By age 13, he had expanded his writing endeavors to include short stories, further honing his skills and overcoming his speech impediment through self-expression.

During his deployment in Iraq, Darrick found solace and inspiration in writing, ultimately birthing the concept for his novel, SierraLeon, along with six additional books. His literary endeavors extended beyond his projects, as he generously shared his talent by crafting love letters, poetry, and proposals for friends.

Darrick's journey from a young boy grappling with a stutter to a prolific writer and veteran is a testament to his resilience, determination, and unwavering commitment to personal growth.